THE MOON CASTS A SPELL

REBECCA LOCHLANN

ERINYES
PRESS

The Moon Casts a Spell
Copyright © Rebecca Lochlann 2014 All rights reserved
Internal design © 2019 Rebecca Lochlann

ISBN-13: 978-0-9982678-2-1
ISBN-10: 0-9982678-2-1
Library of Congress Control Number: 2018908797

Published in the United States by Erinyes Press

Also available as an eBook:
ISBN-10: 0-9838277-7-X
ISBN-13: 978-0-9838277-7-1

Also By Rebecca Lochlann

To Those Caught in Moonspells

THE

MOON

CASTS

A

SPELL

REBECCA LOCHLANN

BOOK FOUR

THE CHILD OF THE ERINYES SERIES

MOTHER

Sections and Dates

"Thou silver deity of secret night…
    My friend, my goddess, and my guide."

~~~ LADY MARY WORTLEY MONTAGU (1689-1762)

The Punishment

November 23,
1853

Chapter

One

LET IT BE DONE.

A wave washed over him, shoved him down where there was no air. He was too tired to fight, and swallowed yet more water. Another swell surged underneath and lifted him to the surface. The waves were like raging dragons, the cold as sharp as knife blades, the water bitter and abrasive against his throat. Sleet pelted his face.

I'm coming, Lilith. We'll be together again. She won't win.

How many more times would he try to convince himself of that, when she had always won, and made every punishment worse than the last?

Claire. Evie. My girls. Forgive me for letting this happen to you.

How could he have so misjudged the hatred?

It doesn't matter anymore.

His mind grew as numb as his body. He couldn't be sure, but he didn't think he was even shivering. He had died four times already, so he wasn't as fearful as someone else might be. Still, the cold was miserable, and it was agonizing to draw salty water into his lungs instead of air. He should open his mouth and drink. Perhaps it would hurry things along.

When his heart stopped, he would drift, one with the waves, and gradually sink. Fish would feast on what was left.

The rising sun broke up the storm clouds. From one horizon to the other, flames covered the heavens. *Red sky at morning, sailors take warning*. His last dawn.

Wait. There was no need for this melodrama. He would see more dawns. He didn't know where or when, but it would start over, the crazed circle of searching, finding, and fighting.

His mind sparked back to life one last time. He saw the murder of his wife and children. He felt the boot soles holding him down, forcing him to watch. He couldn't block out the screams.

We tolerate no witches here!

Just die, he told himself wearily. *Die and be done with it.*

FAINT SHOUTING. COARSE ROPE PASSED AROUND HIS TORSO, UNDER HIS arms. More shouts. Dangling in the air. Thudding hard against unforgiving wood.

Pain and shock brought him back briefly, but he soon drifted away again.

CHOKING, SPUTTERING. A RUSH OF WATER BURNING HIS THROAT, GUSHING from his mouth. Hands shoving hard against his chest.

He retched helplessly.

Some man shouted in his face. "Are you alive?"

"Look at this." Another voice, also male. "Is that a knife wound?"

"It's needing stitches."

"Don't waste the needle and thread. This man won't live another hour."

He floated away.

THE STENCH MADE HIM WISH HE DIDN'T HAVE TO BREATHE. BABIES WAILED without ceasing. He heard moaning, creaking, faraway shouts. Swaying movement rocked him, sometimes gently, sometimes rudely.

His chest radiated blistering pain. He lifted a hand and touched the area, feeling a lumpy wad of cloth.

"You're awake." A face swam into view. Young, bearded, shaggy brown hair. A dirty bandage, edged with dried blood, on the man's cheek.

"Can you tell me your name?"

He blinked. Such noise. It hurt his ears.

"How do you feel?"

He turned away and closed his eyes, but the man didn't leave. Instead he leaned over and adjusted the cloth.

"Just tell me what to call you, and I'll let you sleep. Or I can bring gruel if you're hungry. It's the worst thing you'll ever taste, I warn you."

Leave me be.

"Och. I'll come back later. Rest. I suppose that's what you need most."

HE THRASHED. HE HEARD CHILDREN SCREAMING AND SHRANK FROM THE glint of a knife blade. He dug at his eyes, seeking to gouge them out, and with them, all memory.

Someone had shoved a wet hemp bag, stinking of piss, over his head. He was pushed, kicked, dragged, and thrown into a boat. Much later, several hands hoisted him. Just before he was thrust overboard, he felt something being wrapped around his arm. The sharp tip of a blade slid up his ribs, one by one, then sank into his chest and ripped downward. "Just in case," he heard through his own agonized groans.

The bag was removed and his wrists untied. A soft voice spoke next to his ear. *My father could not save you this time, could he?*

A kick in the spine sent him sprawling into icy water. He fought his way to the surface, choking, hearing the sound of drunken laughter fade as his murderers left him.

He was so cold. He could no longer remember how he came to be in the water, or why.

Da, look at this shell I found. Isn't it pretty? Luminous green eyes full of mystery and magic. A child's arms around his neck. Who was she?

A woman, loosening her glossy dark hair. Sitting on the edge of a bed, crooking her finger. *Show me how Prince Chrysaleon of Mycenae makes love.*

"Wake up, man!" It was that same brown-haired fellow who kept pestering him.

A piercing jolt of pain shot through his head. His throat felt raw. *You killed Daniel. You think you can hide behind your slave?*

"Mother of God! Did you have a bad dream? You're safe. You're safe, I tell you. If you don't stop screaming, you'll bring the captain down on us."

He stopped struggling. Every part of his body ached. The shooting pangs in his head retreated, leaving a dull, repeating throb. "Wh-where am I?"

"You're on the *Bristol*, headed to Nova Scotia. D'you mind what happened? I plucked you out of the ocean."

"O-ocean?"

"Aye, you were half-drowned, but I think you'll survive. There were some wagers on it, I admit."

He could only stare and try to understand what the man was saying. His mind was sluggish, his throat thick and aching. His ears rang and the man's voice echoed.

"Can you at last tell me your name?"

Name?

"What do folk call you, man?"

"I—I don't know." He didn't care, suddenly, where he was, where he was going, if he was alive or dead. He suspected this man had saved his life.

He doubted he would ever forgive that.

The
Boy
From The
Sea

Barra, (Barraigh)
1832
21 years earlier

Chapter

Two

LILITH WAS FEEDING LETTUCE TO THE KIT WHEN A CHANGE IN THE AIR caught her attention. She rose from a squat. There, that unnatural movement of shadow. She squinted into the sunlight, trying to see what it was. Not one figure but two, one shorter than the other, both silhouettes with the sun behind them. The light was blinding, stinging her eyes.

Was that Mam? Something about the outline made her think so. But who was the other?

Inexplicably frightened, she grabbed the kit, holding it tight against her chest, stroking its soft long ears and whispering nonsense.

She watched her father get up from his perch near the front of the cottage, puffing on his pipe. A pungent whiff of smoke drifted her way.

As the approaching figures stepped out of the sunlight and into the shadow thrown by the bulk of the cottage, she blinked, and when her sight adjusted, she saw that it was indeed, her mother, and an unfamiliar boy. Her mother held the boy's hand.

Her mother and father spoke. The boy said nothing, just kept his face pointed at the ground. She couldn't hear what they said, but her father's tone was irritated.

Her mother led the boy over to Lilith. "This is Daniel," she said. "He'll be living with us."

Lilith clutched the kit more tightly. It responded with a protesting squeak and a strong kick of its back legs.

"Can you say something?"

No. Lilith wouldn't even shake her head. She wanted to know why this strange boy was going to live with them. She didn't think she liked it.

The boy squinted at her, revealing brilliant blue eyes and an angry sickle-shaped wound that cut through his left eyebrow, curved around his eye, and ended halfway down his cheek. But before she could properly take in everything about him, he sighed and turned his face down, back to the ground. His shoulders lifted.

He smelled of the sea.

When she'd found the kit, its leg had been bloody and broken, probably from a failed eagle attack.

That boy's glance told her everything. He was wounded, like the kit. Pain rolled off him, an awful sadness that swelled like a cold wave right through her stomach and heart, and lodged in her throat.

She shifted the kit into the crook of her left arm and held out her right hand. Her mother released the boy. Lilith clasped his hand in her own.

He looked up again, his eyes glistening with unshed tears.

Ever since she could remember, she had sung to the sea, and the sea listened. She asked it for a gift, to prove it loved her. This boy was the answer. Her mother must have caught him in a net and was giving him to her to bring back to health.

The sea was there in his eyes—not the cold grey sea that lived in the Outer Hebrides, but a clear blue sea, like a polished stone; the sea as she dreamed it when she stared into the fire at night.

Lilith gave him the kit. He took it carefully. It cuddled against him, lifting its nose to his neck, and he smiled, very faintly.

He would be well and whole again. She would see to it.

Chapter

Three

Stuart watched his wife trudge back to him. His teeth clamped on the stem of his pipe and he sucked in a mouthful of smoke, cursing as he blew it out.

"There's no help for it," Faith said. "You know that."

"I can barely feed those I've already got."

"Claire was my friend. She asked this of me as she died. I could hardly refuse. There's no one else will take him. He's alone in the world now."

"I know that, woman. The others would let him starve, and who's to say that wouldn't be best?"

"I say."

"I wonder if anyone but me realizes what a tender heart you're hiding under all that acid."

"There's a vast difference, I think, between tender-heartedness and common decency."

Giggling drew their attention. Lilith had taken the kit from the boy and put it on the ground. Now both of them were following the creature as it hopped about. Under Lilith's care, the rabbit was growing spoiled and fat. It trailed along after his daughter like a puppy. Stuart knew he'd be feeding that rabbit for as long as it lived, though he'd prefer it in the stew pot feeding him.

Another giggle. Lilith had no patience for anyone or anything but beasts, and she did have a way about her that soothed the wildest, most frightened creature. Stuart watched, astounded, as his daughter put her hand on the boy's forearm. Together they dropped to the ground and took turns holding the kit on their laps. He would have been far less surprised if Lilith ignored the Carson lad, or ran away from him.

Stuart puffed. "She's not right in the head."

"She's fine."

"She says nothing to anybody, but will talk without ceasing to beasts—not a word of which I understand. And the moon—I've caught her talking to the moon. Singing to it even. She's fey. Queer. Maybe a changeling."

"She's not a changeling. She'll come out of it."

"She has no' a single friend. And she should have at least a few words by now."

"She's only five. A bit slow, maybe. You'll see. In another year, she'll be like any other child."

Stuart shivered. He quickly dismissed it as a chill breeze, but he couldn't dismiss his inner conviction so easily.

No, she won't. She'll never be like other children.

The
Factor's
Son

1839

Chapter

Four

Lilith and Daniel sat near the summit of Sheabhal, the tallest hill on Barra, watching the movement of cloud shadows over the islands to the south. They'd been sitting like that for a long time, wordless and content, holding hands.

A boat dropped its sails as it entered the bay and passed the old castle. It drew up beside the rickety wooden pier.

Full of importance, Lilith said, "That's the new factor from Edinburgh. He's going to live at Bishop House, and Mam'll be his housekeeper. I'm to help. She said you'll help too, in the stables."

Daniel shrugged.

"Everybody hates him," she said.

"Already? Why?"

"Because he works for that man—Colonel Gordon, who bought Barraigh. They say he doesn't care about us, just the profits he'll make from our labors. Have you no' heard any of this?"

"I've no use for gossip."

It was true. When folk settled into their beloved conjectures, Daniel went elsewhere—usually someplace with horses. He said gossip always predicted dire events, most of which never happened. Like Lilith, he barely tolerated folk. Maybe that was why they were so close, as close as scales on a fish, Faith often said.

Lilith liked listening to gossip, as long as she wasn't noticed. If she was, she ran away.

"Mam and Da said there will never be MacNeils here again, and that it's bad luck, him selling to an outsider."

"You and I will make our own luck."

"I went along with Mam when they aired the house and polished the furniture," Lilith said. "She wasn't watching, so I sneaked away. Guess what I found?"

"What?" He sounded bored.

"A secret passage!"

Finally. His brows lifted. "A secret passage," he repeated.

"Aye, running all through the house, covered with cobwebs inside. I say nobody's been in there in a hundred years. There are peepholes in every room. In some rooms, there are big square holes, big as windows. Mostly those are covered up though."

"Show me."

"You're daft. Look, they're already off the boat. They'll be at Bishop House before we can get there."

He shrugged. "Doesn't matter. They'll think we're servants. You said we are, anyway."

They raced each other down the steep hill, which served as a comforting backdrop to the village of Castlebay, then diverted east, to the flat summit where Bishop House proudly stood. It was the finest building, if not the oldest, on the entire island of Barra, and overlooked the village and bay like a benevolent patriarch.

As Lilith predicted, the new family arrived before they did. She and Daniel slipped into the kitchen from the rear, hearing the thud of boxes and trunks, scuffling footsteps, and gruff conversation from the front of the house. Some man with an English accent barked instructions, and others, locals, tried to reply in kind, though few on Barra spoke anything but Gaelic.

They entered the corridor, ignored by those who bustled past. Keeping to the shadows, they stopped just outside the big round foyer where everyone was congregated, and stared in at the activity.

An older man, dressed in a fine wool suit, sat in a wheeled wicker Bath chair, a blanket over his legs. A younger fellow, his shirtsleeves rolled up to his elbows, stood beside him, his corded, massive forearms crossed over his chest. Another man, skinny and grooved as a weathered fence post, was attempting to direct the servants. He spoke in English, and was getting red in the face as he struggled to be understood. The man in the Bath chair was pale, his forehead damp with sweat. He coughed repeatedly, and kept a handkerchief pressed to his mouth, only rarely allowing it to drop to his lap.

It wasn't until the Englishman moved away that Lilith saw the boy. He appeared to be about the same age as Daniel, and was standing behind the Bath chair. His hair was black and untidy, disheveled, no doubt from the wind. He, too, was skinny, his face almost as pale as the sick man's. He glowered at the locals who were hauling in the luggage.

She distinctly saw an orange-red glow around him. It made her gasp, as she'd never seen anything like that before—except around Daniel.

He was looking around the foyer, his expression one of arrogance and disdain. When his regard landed on the doorway, his head tilted and he frowned. He left the man in the chair and approached swiftly.

Exchanging a glance, Lilith and Daniel ran back to the kitchens and Lilith led Daniel into a side corridor. She opened one of several doors and yanked him into a musty, dark pantry then down to the floor, where she crawled under a shelf. At the back was a flimsy wood grill, which she pulled off. They slipped into the passageway just as the boy entered the corridor. He paused at the open door.

"You'd better come out," he shouted. They saw his boots, very shiny and clean, but he didn't enter the pantry. Lilith and Daniel exchanged another glance and Lilith put her hand over her mouth to keep from giggling as the boy closed the door and went on down the hallway.

Chapter

Five

THEY CRAWLED ALONG, LOOKING THROUGH PEEPHOLES INTO VARIOUS rooms. Only two of the larger openings were free of coverings. The first they came to fairly quickly, high on the wall in one of the drawing rooms. It offered a dim view through iron latticework of the fireplace, tables with lace runners, several chairs, and two plush loveseats.

Eventually they came to the other window-like opening that wasn't blocked by a painting or tapestry. They peered through the scrolled ironwork into a bedroom. Two men carried in a trunk and set it on the floor. Another brought in several leather bags. The boy they'd hidden from entered then, and impatiently motioned for the men to leave. When they'd gone, he shut the door and removed his coat and cravat, tossing them carelessly onto the bed. He started rolling up his shirt-sleeves.

Lilith, forgetting to be careful, released a nervous giggle. Daniel clapped a hand over her mouth but it was too late. The tight space magnified the sound, hushed though it was, and it rebounded outward through the iron grating.

The boy came forward and ripped the cover off even as Daniel pulled at Lilith. The boy reached into the hole; seizing Lilith's skirts, he dragged her out roughly. Daniel followed without hesitation. Dropping to the floor, he put himself between the boy and Lilith, raising his fists.

The boy stared as though he'd never seen a girl in his life. Then, without warning, a sickly green hue tinged his face. "Aridela," he whispered.

He slumped against Daniel and slid to the floor.

Lilith and Daniel stared at each other and at the boy. "They'll hang us for murder!" Lilith said, her voice shaking.

The more practical Daniel knelt, pressing his fingers to the boy's throat. "He's alive. Help me."

With much struggling, they managed to hoist him onto his bed. Lilith brought over the washbasin and patted his face with water, all the while muttering, "Please wake up, please." He was definitely breathing, though. With a hint of derision, Daniel said, "He fainted, that's all. Let's away now while we can."

"No." The boy wasn't well and she wouldn't leave him. He was no different than any other beast she'd rescued or nursed. She pulled off his boots and tucked a blanket over him.

He woke slowly, blinking. Some semblance of color returned to his face. He glanced around the room in a puzzled manner, frowning, but as he studied Lilith, his gaze narrowed. He squinted and grabbed her forearms. Daniel pushed between them, again raising a fist, but before he could make any threats, the boy said, "I saw colors coming out of the wall. I felt like I was on fire."

Lilith nodded. "I saw colors around you. I can see them right now."

The boy finally tore his gaze from Lilith and looked at Daniel. "You, too," he said, but his voice turned colder and his chin lifted.

"I've never seen color around anyone but Daniel," Lilith said.

Daniel, refusing to be drawn in, said, "If you're recovered, we'll be off."

"Wait," said the boy. "Who are you?"

Lilith and Daniel glanced at each other, able as usual to communicate without words. What if he had them punished for being in the wall staring at him? He could get her mother in trouble, too.

"Fiona and John, from the village. We were hired to help."

"You're lying," the boy said. "You just called him 'Daniel.' If you don't tell me the truth, I'll make sure neither of you ever finds work again. You know who my father is—the new factor. He'll be collecting rents and overseeing everything, disputes, complaints, problems. You don't want to cross me."

"I'm the housekeeper's daughter. My name is Lilith." She didn't look at Daniel. "Don't blame my mother. She doesn't know what we were doing."

"Lilith," the boy repeated, and his lips turned up in a slight smile. His grip on her forearms remained unrelenting, but his thumbs rubbed back and forth on the inside of her wrists, almost like a caress, and odd, zipping charges, like sparks of fire, leapt into her flesh where his fingers touched. "Wayward Lilith, Adam's first wife. Of course."

"I'm not married," she said, "and I don't know anyone named Adam."

"She's only eleven," Daniel said, scowling.

The boy's faint smile lingered. "How is it you speak English?"

"My mam's a schoolteacher," she said. "Being your housekeeper pays more though."

He looked down and saw the birthmark on her wrist, the odd blemish shaped like a bull's head with horns. She flushed and tried to pull her hand free, but he held on, tracing the perimeter of it.

"Let go of her." Daniel pried at the boy's hands. "Let us get back to our chores."

"Damn you," the boy said. "Daniel, is it? I'll call in my father's man."

"Aye, he's Daniel," Lilith said, scared and believing his threat. "He —he's an orphan. He'll be working in your stables. He's good with horses. He's my friend."

Daniel flushed.

Anger darkened the boy's eyes, making his countenance as black as the Devil's. "Be off with you then, and don't let me catch you in my walls again, or you'll rue it, and so will your mother."

Chapter

Six

When they were safely away, Daniel ridiculed the wealthy, nose-in-the-air boy with the clean fingernails, fine accent, and blindingly white cravat.

"He's never done a day's labor," Daniel said. Lilith heard under his words how relieved he was that nothing worse had happened.

Lilith couldn't get the boy's face out of her mind, or how he stared so intensely as he stroked her wrists. He'd sparked her protective instincts when he dropped to the floor. What caused him to faint that way? Was he ill? He'd called her that other name. She couldn't remember it now.

Something about his voice made her think of the sea.

She couldn't decide how she felt about him at all.

Faith took Lilith every day to help with the cleaning and cooking at Bishop House. Daniel usually came along to muck the stables and brush the fine horses brought by the new steward.

Aodhàn was the boy's name. Aodhàn Mackinnon. Kenneth Mackinnon was the sickly man in the wheeled chair. He was Aodhàn's consumptive father. The lout with the massive shoulders and arms was Kenneth Mackinnon's valet, Euan Kilgore. Finally, there was the lanky Englishman, Greyson Fullerton, who was a combination valet, orderly, manservant, and tutor to Aodhàn. A family of men, all of them expert at scowling.

For a fortnight after the confrontation, Lilith didn't see Aodhàn except from a distance. Every now and then, she glimpsed that faint reddish haze of color around him, but it faded with the passage of time. She seldom saw colors around Daniel anymore either, except at night, when she slipped out of the cot to relieve herself or check on one of her rescued beasts. His was bluish white, like the sea on bright, cloudless days. Back when he'd first come to live with them, he'd told her she was surrounded by a wash of purple, like what seeped through the sky at deepest gloaming, and hints of sparkly gold. Early on they'd figured out that no one else ever saw these colors. It was another reason they latched themselves together and didn't bother making friends with the other village children.

Now someone else had come along who could see it. Lilith knew this was important. It didn't matter that Aodhàn was wealthy, educated, a mainlander, as far removed from them as if he were the son of a king.

Twice she caught Aodhàn speaking with her mother when no one else was about, and once she thought she saw him hand Faith a gold coin. She couldn't imagine what Faith and the steward's young son would have in common, or what he could be paying her for. Both times they fell silent when they saw her. Aodhàn went off with a nod, and her mother never shared whatever it was they spoke of together, or that he'd given her anything, much less money.

Furniture and other belongings arrived from the mainland. Bishop House became an elegant, lively, busy place, hosting friends, relatives, and business acquaintances. But as far as Lilith knew, the actual new owner of their island, a Colonel from Aberdeen or somewhere, who went by the name of John Gordon of Cluny, never came, not once, to inspect his holdings or meet his tenants.

In April, the family celebrated Aodhàn's birthday, but nobody said how old he was.

Faith sent Lilith to clean the fireplace in the main parlor early one morning in May, telling her to be quick so she'd be done and gone by the time the family went in there.

She took care with the task, sweeping up every last bit of ash and polishing the brass knobs on the grate, humming as she worked. When she was finished, she gathered up her bucket and brushes and rose.

Aodhàn was standing next to the door, watching her. She was so startled she released a cry and almost dropped the bucket. Then she remembered what her mother had told her to do in such a case. She bobbed a brief curtsy and tried to pass by him, but he took hold of her arm. Even through her sleeve she felt that same sparking excitement, like tiny bursts of lightning, passing from him into her.

"Don't go," he said, pulling her back into the room. He dropped into one of the armchairs in front of the fireplace and stared at her. His eyes were very green, like sunlight through a leaf.

"You stare at me so," Lilith blurted. "Have I done something—something *else*—wrong?"

"No," Aodhàn said. "Sit there. I want to get to know you."

She obediently perched on the edge of the chair he indicated, keeping her hands curled into fists on her lap because they were dirty.

"How old did that boy say you are?" he finally asked.

"Eleven—how old are you?"

"Thirteen."

She'd thought him closer to Daniel's age, which was fifteen. Maybe it was his arrogance, his confidence, that made him appear older. She twisted her fingers together and glanced at the door.

"How did you feel, the first time you saw me?" he asked.

How did she feel? What a question. But then, as she thought back to that moment she'd seen him in the foyer at Bishop House, it wasn't so odd.

"Like I'd been hit by lightning." Her mother often reprimanded her for being too blunt, though she herself was exactly that way. Lilith hadn't spoken to anyone until Daniel came to live with them when she was five, and rarely spoke to anyone except him for several years, but after she did begin to talk, it seemed like she was always being chastised for saying the wrong thing.

The boy smiled. "So did I."

His voice wrapped her in warmth, like a soft blanket.

She leaped up, dropping her fireplace brush. "I—I should go, sir."

He leaned forward and retrieved the brush. He held it out, but didn't release it when she tried to take it from him.

"You and I," he said, so low she was able to tell herself later that she'd misunderstood. "For as long as the pyramids stand in Egypt."

She tugged until he let go of the brush. Keeping her face lowered, she picked up her bucket and left, feeling his gaze follow her like a wolf on the hunt.

OVER THE NEXT SEVERAL MONTHS, AODHÀN APPEARED WHENEVER SHE WAS working alone. She often caught him watching when she was with other servants, but he never approached her at those times.

Daniel eventually noticed, too. He warned Lilith to be careful. He candidly told her Aodhàn would take her virginity then have nothing more to do with her. He said that if the opportunity arose, the factor's son might even attack her.

When she refused to make any promises, he said something she knew he wasn't ready to say. His saying it proved how frightened he was.

"You and I will marry someday. It's always been understood. Your da even said so. I have his blessing. You're mine, Lilith. Don't get any daft ideas about the manky bastard in the big house."

Lilith exploded. "I don't want to get married! I don't belong to you. Just because we took you in to keep you from starving doesn't mean you have any right to me!"

He went pale and she ran off to the hills, to her wind and the thunder of the sea. It was the only place she felt right.

But after a few hours, guilt consumed her. Of course she would marry Daniel. Everybody knew it. It had never been said—it didn't need to be said.

Why did Aodhàn Mackinnon have to come to Barra? Why couldn't he leave her alone? Why did he have to make her feel so strange, tingly and nervous, hot and cold?

Chapter

Seven

"I WANT YOU TO GO BACK TO BISHOP HOUSE FOR ME," FAITH SAID TO HER daughter one late afternoon in early September. "I took my mending bag with me this morning and I must have left it there. Run fetch it for me, lass."

"I'll go with you," Daniel said, but Faith stopped him. "She doesn't need your help to get my mending, and Stuart wants those rotted ropes in the thatch fixed."

He frowned and started to say something, then didn't.

Lilith knew why. Daniel never forgot what he owed Faith and Stuart Kelso; he never allowed himself to argue with them, as a natural born child might. Stuart had been asking him to replace the frayed ropes on the roof for a fortnight. It had to be done soon, else they risked losing their entire roof in the winter gales. Daniel had told her he wanted to wait and do it at the same time as they pulled down the old oat straw and replaced it with new, but Stuart apparently had other ideas. Either that, or Faith simply didn't want him going to Bishop House with Lilith.

Since the fight with Daniel, Lilith had been careful to avoid any interaction with Aodhàn, though in her heart she felt as though she were a fish and he the fisherman, with a hook lodged in her throat. She wanted to learn more about him, what his life had been up until now. She wanted to lie in the hills with her eyes closed and listen to his voice, which possessed something, a timbre that sent shivers over her skin. She wanted to feel his fingers stroke her wrists again.

Humans were incomprehensible most of the time. She couldn't even understand herself, much less any others. She much preferred beasts; they were always the same, simple and direct.

Daniel's fear made her feel like she was looking out at the world from inside a birdcage. Why would someone cage a bird, prevent it from flying free? But the long history between them left her torn. She didn't want to do anything to hurt him.

With this in mind, she slipped quietly into the rear entry of Bishop House. Faith had told her she'd left the bag in the sitting room off the kitchen. Lilith went quickly along the corridor and opened the door to the chamber.

No lamps were lit but a fire burned in the fireplace. The second thing she noticed was Aodhàn, sitting in one of two stuffed chairs. She had a feeling, when he looked up at her, that he'd known she was coming.

"Excuse me, sir," she said, and backed out. But he was up in a flash, laying his hand on her arm and drawing her into the room, which was filled with shifting light and shadow from the fire.

"I'm leaving in two days for Eton," he said. "Who knows when or if we will ever see each other again? I only want to say goodbye."

Daniel's warnings echoed, but they grew fainter and fainter as Aodhàn leveled his intense gaze on her and gestured for her to sit in the other chair.

"I have a gift for you." Reaching into his coat pocket, he brought out a square of material and placed it in her hand.

She unfolded it and drew in a breath. A pendant winked up at her, shining like the sea did sometimes, in certain light—like liquid silver, the sheen enhanced by the soft black velvet he'd wrapped it in. In the center was a luminous blue bead, tucked between two crescent moons. It was an elegant, beautifully carved thing. "I cannot take this," she whispered. "It is too dear."

"I want you to have it." He hooked his index finger under the chain and suspended it so the firelight reflected against its face. She couldn't stop herself from reaching out. The instant she touched it, something bolted through her from scalp to toes. She gasped. The hair on the back of her neck prickled. A bit of dry wood in the fire sparked, causing the face of the pendant to momentarily dazzle and blind her. Her ears reverberated with a deafening hum and she tasted something on her tongue like cold, cold earth and rock. She had a strange sense that starlight, trapped within the silver, had pierced her skin and infiltrated her blood.

"It's very old," he said.

She lifted her gaze to his. "How old?"

"Very, very old. There's a story. Would you like to hear it?"

"Aye." She placed the necklace on her palm, allowing its silver chain to dangle freely.

"The necklace belonged to a queen in a faraway country, in a time so long ago all memory of it is lost. Her palace is buried now under sand and dirt, and those who walk upon it have no idea it was ever there. But this palace, filled with gold, obsidian, and lapis, its walls covered in bright paintings, its corridors adorned with marble statues, was once the envy of every other land."

Lilith nodded. She had many questions, but she didn't want to disrupt his thoughts.

"The people called it *Labyrinthos*—the labyrinth—for it was a common boast that there were as many rooms as there are stars in the heavens, more underground than above. It was a marvel to behold, and the island where it was located was the only realm left in the world to be ruled by women."

Lilith's breath caught. How did he do it? How did he tell a story that hearkened straight to her dreams?

"A catastrophe befell the island. Everything was destroyed. Everything. But the queen, who was beautiful and wise, courageous and loyal, led her people back from death and horror. She found food and medicines for the injured. She and her warriors fought off invaders. With time, she rebuilt her palace; her land again became fertile. The gods were appeased."

Lilith felt as if she were there, inside his fanciful tale. At the edge of her vision she saw sunlight reflecting off gold, and enormous crimson pillars. The dreary real things of her world—hunger, shabby clothing, packed earth floors, a home shared with kye and sheep, fell away. She didn't care that night had fallen, or that she was alone with the boy—a young man, really. She wished to be nowhere else.

"The necklace was crafted in a legendary pool, a secret cavern where the moon went into hiding when it disappeared from the skies. Though the queen is long dead, her great civilization lost, the necklace goes on casting her spell, century after century, for within it is forged the amaranthine light of the moon."

Not starlight then. Moonlight. Lilith ran the tip of her index finger over the face of the pendant. The exhilarating energy had faded. She barely felt a tingle flit through her skin. But when she looked up at Aodhàn, the colors she'd glimpsed when he'd first come to Bishop House had returned. Like a wisp of cloud, like the soft exhalation of a breath, they hovered, swirling, a suggestion of deep red blending into streaks of orange.

She wondered what *amaranthine* meant.

Gradually, she realized he'd stopped talking, yet somehow it felt as though they were still communicating. Pictures rose and fell within her mind, of strange, foreign places and faceless people.

He rose from his chair. Clasping her wrists, he drew her to her feet. He was close, so close she felt the warmth of his flesh and saw each individual eyelash framing his eyes. A muscle was leaping beneath the skin under his left eye. His right thumb gently rubbed the birthmark.

"Promise you'll keep the necklace until I come back," he said. "Will you?"

"Aye."

"It's a secret, just between us. Tell no one else. Show it to no one. Do you promise?"

"Aye."

She knew what he would do next. She saw it in his eyes. He had to bend down, as he was much taller than she. He kissed her on the mouth.

She'd never been kissed before. Daniel had only kissed her on the cheek, on Christmas morning or her birthday. Her mother never kissed anyone, not even her father, so far as Lilith knew.

Her eyes closed, allowing her to better experience these new sensations.

"Forget about Daniel, Lilith," he whispered. "You are going to marry me."

It was so similar to what Daniel had said about him that it shattered the spell. She sucked in a deep breath and opened her eyes, suddenly lightheaded. The room was dancing—it took a moment to realize it was an illusion caused by the firelight.

He left her then, after brushing back her hair and smiling down into her face.

She dropped onto the chair, too weak and shivery to go on standing. She felt like a pebble in a gushing burn, swept along without any choice in the matter.

But Lilith was not like other girls. She didn't feel as though she was going to weep, or faint away with "vapors." She was clear-headed. Her mind registered her excitement. She wanted to give herself to the rushing water, to spin and keel, to become a part of its inexorable power.

She tried to make no sound when she entered the cottage, but Daniel must have been waiting. He opened his eyes when she came in and stared at her.

She tightened her grip on the necklace in her pocket and went off to the alcove that held her pallet, along with her parents'. Her mother, she saw with a glance, was also awake and watching.

Where Daniel's gaze had been suspicious and angry, Faith's, illuminated by the light of a single candle, was speculative.

Lilith blew out the candle and climbed into her bed. She held the necklace all night.

Daniel Courts his Sweetheart

February, 1845

Chapter

Eight

DANIEL HADN'T FORMALLY ASKED LILITH TO MARRY HIM, THOUGH HE'D turned twenty-one and Lilith was a fully marriageable seventeen. He was Kenneth Mackinnon's head groom now, respected, liked, trusted with the man's beloved horses; still, he didn't feel he could support a wife, and certainly not a wife, her mother, and future offspring.

Stuart Kelso had died at sea two years back, and Daniel had taken over as man of the house. He often worked two or three fees besides his obligations at Bishop House, when he could get them, as he tried to keep his women in comfort. Lately he'd bandied about the idea of emigrating to Canada, if he could find a way to pay the cost of the voyage for the three of them.

He was so busy he hardly ever thought of Aodhàn Mackinnon. The factor's son had been gone a long while, near on six years, being educated in England. Every once in a while he came back for short visits, but kept himself scarce when he did. Daniel had no reason to be jealous, and indeed believed Aodhàn's youthful infatuation with Lilith had dissolved with the passage of time. No doubt he'd been introduced to many higher-born, sophisticated women made even more enticing by the generous dowries that would accompany them into marriage.

But Daniel never took anything for granted, and kept up with his courting. Every day he brought Lilith a gift, sometimes a bracelet woven from wildflowers he'd gathered from the machair, or a pretty shell from the beach, or a trinket he dug up at one of the ancient places he and Lilith loved to explore. A year or so ago he'd found a ring of bronze. He'd taken it to the blacksmith, who used a paste of flour, vinegar, and salt to polish away the patina and corrosion. The blacksmith made it smaller and inscribed it at Daniel's request with their names and a wee heart. Daniel had it in his pocket now.

"Daniel!"

Lilith was climbing the slope, holding up her skirts in front to keep from tripping. He descended to meet her and took her hand, assisting her to the summit of the ridge, where they admired the sea and kissed. She wrapped her arms around his neck and pressed against him, wordlessly asking for more as she often did. No matter how many times he tried to explain it, Lilith couldn't understand the importance of female purity. She wanted what she wanted, like one of her wild creatures, like a dolphin in the deep green ocean.

"No, love," he said, though refusing her was growing more and more difficult. "We'll wait till we're married, my Lilith, it's the only way. I would never cheat you of that."

"Marry me now. The sea can be our witness. Or look—there's a seal. It can oversee the ceremony."

He laughed. "First I must find a way to give you a decent life—you, your mother, and our children."

"You're Kenneth Mackinnon's head groom. You earn coin enough. He likes you. I'd wager if you told him you wanted to marry, he'd give you a bonus."

"I don't want to work for him," Daniel said. "I'll find something else—something far from here."

He brought the ring from his pocket and held it out on his palm.

"Oh, what is it?" she cried.

"It's for you."

"It has our names! And a heart." She held it up to the light.

"Here." He slipped it on her finger. "A promise, until we can be together forever. I found it over at Allt Easdail. It's thousands of years old, that's what I think, like the love between us."

"Oh, Daniel," she whispered, and melted against him again, kissing his cheeks, his mouth, his neck. "That's true. I've always known it. I didn't know you did, though."

"Stop it," he said, laughing. "I am not made of stone, you know." Bringing a leather strap out of his other pocket, he put the ring on it and fastened the thong around her neck. "We'll keep it a secret just for now. I don't want to hear Faith's opinions. I've always known she wants better for you than me."

"Aye, that's wise," she agreed, and tucked it under her blouse.

He held her then, burying his nose in her hair. Lilith's scent was a natural aphrodisiac, a musky, earthy essence he loved. "You make me feel I can achieve anything," he said against her skin.

They both noticed the lone figure as they descended the hill and set off on the trail through the machair that would take them home. When the man saw them looking at him, he walked swiftly away.

"Greyson Fullerton," Daniel said darkly. "Why does he watch us?"

Lilith shrugged, drawing the ring out from under her blouse so she could admire it. "The poor man is far from his homeland, and there's precious little to do on Barra. I wonder why he stays on? He was tutor to Aodhàn—" she stopped and sent Daniel an anxious glance, but he smiled and squeezed her hand, so she went on. "Mackinnon, and he's no longer needed for that."

"Lilith, did he ever…try anything with you?"

"He kissed me," she said after a long pause. "Once. Before he went away."

A lava flow of rage flooded him before he realized they were speaking of something six years in the past. He ran a hand through his hair and laughed at himself. "He may come back one day," he said.

She shrugged. "Why would he? There's nothing for him here."

"His father."

"By the time he finishes at Oxford, he'll be a full-grown man, and I'm sure he'll want much grander things than the Western Isles can provide."

"At last, you admit there's no future here! Can we all go to Canada now?"

Aodhàn Comes Home

March,
1845

Chapter

Nine

It didn't take long for gossip to start circulating after Faith gave birth to Lilith.

The word *changeling* was bandied about before she was two years old, but such mean-spirited talk was kept from Faith. She had a renowned temper; it was said her tongue could slice bacon from a sow before it could utter a shriek in protest.

There was nothing obviously wrong about Lilith. Yet the crofters and fishwives of Barra sensed differences. Where other children experienced joy in small things, Lilith frowned, and was unnaturally quiet. Once or twice Faith said the wean was lucky not to starve to death, for she never cried to let her mother know she was hungry, and there had been a few times where Faith simply forgot to feed her and change her hippins.

From the youngest age, Lilith babbled to animals and they to her, but when humans tried to get her to speak, she wouldn't.

Not until Daniel came.

Seven days after he moved into their blackhouse, the two could be seen running across the dunes and bluffs holding hands. Some claimed they'd heard Lilith speaking to Daniel as clearly and unmistakably as could be, but if she realized others were listening, she shut her mouth like a mussel.

Daniel became her voice in the world. It was Daniel's job to explain her to others. Four years older than she, Daniel was as protective as any natural older brother had ever been—perhaps more so. She was seldom out of his earshot, so no one molested her. In her mother's schoolroom, she never said a word yet her brain obviously worked, for she could write with the best in the class, and even picked up the English, or so it was rumored, anyway.

She seldom displayed emotion, except when she was confined. In the schoolroom, Faith learned to ignore it if Lilith got up, left, and didn't return. Trying to force her to follow rules, to sit quietly, to stay inside, could cause unearthly tantrums. Even Daniel couldn't calm her when she fought being restrained. Once, when a storm blew hard enough that it came close to tearing the stone-weighted ropes from the roof and the family nearly lost their thatch, she wrestled with the door trying to get out. Her father trussed her in his arms by the fire, but she screamed and twisted and hit him until he gave up and let her go. She didn't return all that night, and her mother fell silent, believing her daughter had frozen to death on the bluffs.

But Daniel didn't worry, and when she came back the next day, she was no worse for wear.

"Found some rat hole," Stuart said. "They let her in, no doubt, and fed her too."

"I WANT HIM DEAD."

Shaking out one of Aodhàn's shirts, Greyson Fullerton straightened. "Pardon?"

"You heard me."

Greyson pulled several more shirts from the trunk. "Lure her away from him, my lord. You have done it before."

"It's gone on too long this time." Aodhàn threw himself into the chair by the window and rubbed his forehead. "Why do you think I'm here?"

"My last letter?"

"You said they are secretly betrothed."

"I suspect it's a matter of finance that keeps them from announcing it. But, my lord, you're tired from your long journey. You'll feel differently when you've rested. What you suggest is drastic, and I do not need to remind you that you'd be prevented, or punished—if not by these people, then by...*her*."

Greyson's words brought back an ancient memory, one that returned to Aodhàn from time to time. He was in the labyrinth on Crete, seeking the bull leaper, Lycus. He had to kill the youth so he could become king. He'd been making his way through darkness, stumbling, cursing, and had heard a voice.

You will follow.

He'd swung his sword blade wildly, thinking someone was there in that darkness with him.

Without any change in inflection, the disembodied voice had added, *But when you ask it, you will have my forgiveness.*

He often wondered if the voice had been no more than delusion, his mind creating things because of the darkness, or the drugs he'd been given, or his own fear. But some part of him knew the goddess he hated had been there, watching. Listening. The memory still made his flesh shiver.

You will have my forgiveness.

Or I will win! He sent the defiant thought outward even as he said, mildly, "That's why you will do it for me."

"Me?" Greyson bent to the task of inspecting a pair of riding boots and brushing off a bit of dust, but Aodhàn heard the tremble in his voice.

"I've thought it all out. I will make some excuse and take Father to Mingulay—for the air, to force him to rest. I'll insist that Faith and Lilith go with us. I want it done by the time we return."

Greyson set the boots in the wardrobe and faced Aodhàn. "Don't ask me to do this."

Aodhàn tapped his knee. "You're refusing?"

"I will always do whatever you require. But I feel in my bones we must not. He is your brother, my lord."

"He was my brother, a long time ago. Now he's a thorn in my side, always using her loyalty against me."

"Remember Crete, and Cape—"

"Damn you, I don't need your reminders. I've lost six years. She'll escape me if I don't do something."

"Why didn't you try harder to win her before now? You haven't done a thing on your visits—avoided her, even."

"Because I know what she responds to. If I pushed her it would make things worse. Keeping my distance has lodged me in her mind like a wasp."

Movement outside the window drew Aodhàn's attention. Daniel was leading one of his father's horses from the stable. The stallion was restless, bobbing its head, prancing and jerking against the lead, but Daniel didn't force his will upon it. He stepped closer and put his hand on the beast's nose. It responded by quieting, swishing its tail and nudging Daniel's shoulder. Daniel released it in the paddock and observed it for a moment as it galloped and bucked, then he glanced up at Aodhàn's window like he knew he was being watched.

Aodhàn's teeth clenched.

FᴀɪTH ʀᴇᴍᴏᴠᴇᴅ ʜᴇʀ sʜᴀᴡʟ, ғᴏʟᴅᴇᴅ ɪᴛ, ᴀɴᴅ ᴅʀᴀᴘᴇᴅ ɪᴛ ᴏᴠᴇʀ ᴛʜᴇ ʙᴀᴄᴋ ᴏғ the rocking chair. "The master's son is home," she said.

Though Lilith was at the hearth tending the stew and Daniel was off in the shadows milking the goat, she sensed him stiffen.

She said nothing; she didn't even look at her mother. She kept her head down and stirred their supper as she contemplated how she'd known this for days, known he was coming closer.

"Greyson tells me he won't be going back for a while," Faith added into the sudden, tense silence. "Due to his father's health."

Lilith tried to dampen the thrill surging like a tide swell through her blood. Carefully, she took the cauldron from its hook and set it on the table, turning to fetch bowls and spoons. Daniel's gaze, and his thoughts, pummeled her as he walked across the room, carrying a bucket of milk, which he added to the table.

"He has been getting worse," Lilith said tonelessly. She gestured; Faith and Daniel sat down and she joined them, ladling stew into bowls. "Sometimes I have to repeat what I've read three or four times because of his coughing."

"I wonder why John Gordon hired such a sick man to oversee this place," Faith said. "There must be a debt of some kind. Does Master Kenneth ever bring him up?"

Lilith shook her head. "The Colonel? Only in passing." She remembered Aodhàn, the thin, black-headed, intense boy. She knew from his father that he'd left Eton and was now at Oxford. She'd hardly seen him during the last six years. His most recent visit had been over a year ago. When he had been here, he'd kept his distance. Now, hearing he was home and apparently meant to stay, her mind leaped with old images and memories. *Forget about Daniel. You are going to marry me.*

She swallowed a mouthful of stew and kept a neutral expression. Had he forgotten that vow, made when he was a boy? What did he look like now? Had he changed?

"Did you hear me, girl?"

"What?"

"I said you're to come with me tomorrow and help with the cooking. They're expecting guests from the mainland."

Lilith glanced at Daniel. He was frowning, staring narrowly at her throat. She realized she'd pulled the ring he'd given her out from beneath her blouse. Quickly, she put it back where it belonged. "As you please," she said, and shifted the conversation to what they would be preparing, and for how many.

THE SECRET PASSAGEWAY WAS TIGHTER THAN LILITH REMEMBERED. THERE was so much dust she had to stifle three sneezes before she reached Aodhàn's bedroom.

She took her time, careful to make no sound whatsoever as she neared the lattice-covered opening in his wall. If he discovered her this time, she would die of embarrassment, not to mention the wrath she might bring down on herself, her mother, and Daniel. She was no longer a wean, who could be forgiven for exploring the nooks and crannies of a big house. She'd argued with herself about it all day as she'd performed the duties asked of her: peeling potatoes, slicing leeks, and basting the lamb. Every now and then she glanced at the hallway where the pantries were situated. No one had ever mentioned finding the passageway. She suspected its location, on the floor, underneath a shelf, back in a dusty dark corner, effectively kept it secret.

The perfect moment came when Faith and Sarah Lamont went out to the kailyard in search of pretty garnishes. Lilith slipped into the passage, hoping it would be as easy to get back into the kitchen when she'd finished spying on the master's son. Though she was still skinny, it was much harder to squeeze beneath the shelf than it had been six years ago.

She peered into the room from her hiding place. He was lying on the bed, dressed in dark trousers and a spotless white shirt, open at the neck. His long, elegant fingers gripped the edges of an open book. He frowned as he read and she saw his jaw clench, a jaw shadowed with stubble, as though he hadn't shaved in a day or so.

It struck her hard as he turned a page. The boy who had flirted with her was gone. The figure on the bed was in every way a man.

Seeing the changes, some subtle, others palpable, made her wonder about her own. Would she look different to him now? Would he notice? Did he even remember her?

A startled *eek* emerged from her throat when he said, "It's dirty and damp in there. Come out." He turned another page then patted the bed beside him.

She lay there, wishing she knew a way to disintegrate into dust motes.

"Come, Lilith." One brow lifted and he sent her a slight, challenging smile. "Or are you afraid?"

Gritting her teeth, she put her fingers through the holes in the latticework and pushed it off the wall, letting it clatter to the floor. She was caught. She may as well accept it. And no one could call her afraid with impunity.

He came over to the wall, holding up his hands to help her into the room.

She dropped out of the hole, stumbling a little when her shoe struck a framed painting that was propped against the wall. She looked up and saw the nail embedded above the hole. He'd removed it. Was it because he hoped she might come through the passageway?

He'd put one hand on her waist and there it remained. He gazed at her every bit as intensely as he had when he was thirteen. She felt her cheeks burn, partly because she'd been caught spying on him, partly because he was making her feel like her hair had come undone or her skirt was up around her knees. No doubt she was covered in dust.

His grip on her waist tightened and he waltzed her around the room. "Every sound you make in that passageway is concentrated by the way it's shaped," he said. "Even breathing. No matter how quiet you try to be, I will always know you're there."

She looked away from his laughing eyes, wishing she could dunk her head in ice water. The book he'd been reading lay open on the bed; it drew a second glance from her, because, while some of the letters looked familiar, others did not. Some resembled triangles, there was a sideways placed M, one looked like a horseshoe, and there was an O with an I slicing vertically through it. "What is that?" she asked, refusing to take another step.

"Sappho," he said. Seeing her confusion, he added, "A Greek poet."

"You read Greek." Somehow this fact made her realize, as his fine clothing and surroundings never had, just how removed he truly was from her.

"You have grown up." He brought her hand to his mouth and kissed it.

So have you, she managed to keep herself from saying. She wrenched her hand free and it went, instinctively, to Daniel's ring on the thong around her neck.

Aodhàn frowned. He pried her hand off the ring. When he saw what it was, he scowled. His accusatory gaze lifted to hers. "Daniel's ring? I told you to forget about him." The tic she remembered seeing once before pulsed under his eye.

"Who are you to tell me what to do? I've known Daniel my whole life. You're nobody to us. Nobody! You'll get bored here and move to Edinburgh or London. You don't fool me."

He pulled on the thong, forcing her closer. Her eyes narrowed. "Don't break it," she said in warning.

He was so close she almost felt consumed. His gaze was like a predator's. There was tense silence, before he released the thong and stepped back. He smiled and bowed. "Grown up in more ways than one," he said, glancing over her figure. "A formidable woman."

She heard the respect in his voice and felt she had won a small battle. Still, she had been caught spying on him, which was mortifying. That fact tempered her victory. "Mam will be looking for me. I'm supposed to be helping cook your dinner."

"Then why leave your work and come through the passage?" he asked softly.

He advanced again, putting his hands on her shoulders, backing her against the wall. She felt the chill of the passageway waft against the back of her neck. His proximity made her realize how much taller he was. His eyes were on her mouth, and his hands gripped her collar; she wondered if he meant to rip it.

"No," she whispered fiercely, not sure if she spoke to him or herself. Her heart was hammering.

He stopped, his lips almost touching hers. She felt the heat of him, the warmth of his breath, his knuckles against her throat. He moved a little so he could press his nose in her hair. "I've missed the scent of you," he said, which was odd. She knew she smelled of dust and cooking food.

Then he brought his mouth next to hers. "I will never force you. I don't have to. You will come to me."

"No I won't," she replied, giving every effort to speaking with conviction. "Never."

With the quickest, lightest kiss against the corner of her mouth he retreated. Lifting a hand, he stroked her cheek with his knuckles then left the room.

She exhaled, unclenched her hands, and tried to dispel the heat and elevated heartbeat, the betraying response she felt everywhere, his *Aye, you will,* echoing in her mind.

Chapter

Ten

"MASTER AODHÀN IS TAKING HIS FATHER TO MINGULAY," FAITH SAID over breakfast. "Something about the air. We're to go along and keep house. Sarah Lamont is going as well, to do the cooking."

"What?" Daniel shouted. "No!"

Faith, in her inimitable way, merely lifted a brow. "And who are you to say what I do, and my daughter? I work for Kenneth Mackinnon. If I'm told to go to Mingulay to keep his house, that's what I'll be doing. I don't have the luxury of refusing, if I want to eat."

Swallowing, lowering his voice, he said, "Lilith isn't needed. Surely you know why he wants her there."

Faith didn't reply for a moment, nor did her expression betray shock or denial. "Lilith has worked at Bishop House by my side for the last six years, and no harm has come to her. Kenneth Mackinnon likes her to read to him. He says her voice is soothing. I don't know what you're thinking, but I will be there to watch over her."

"I'll go along," he said quickly.

She scoffed. "They're not bringing horses. You aren't needed." Taking a last sip of tea, she rose from the table. "You've lived with us a long time, and maybe you think that gives you a say, but it doesn't. I don't answer to you, Daniel Carson."

Lilith watched Daniel's hands clench as well as his jaw, but he said nothing. He turned his gaze from Faith to Lilith. She smiled at him reassuringly, and unobtrusively caressed the ring he'd given her.

Aodhàn had only been home five days, and already had thrown their usually uneventful lives into chaos.

The next morning, Daniel found Lilith in their usual spot, the hills along the east coast. He took her hand.

"I can't let you go," he said. "I know why Aodhàn Mackinnon is taking you. Men of privilege think they can do anything they want, no matter what harm it causes others. If you go, Lilith, everyone will say he's had you, whether it's true or not."

"Not with my mother there, and Sarah Lamont. Kenneth Mackinnon will be there too, and he doesn't want his son trifling with the servants. Mam is right—we have no choice, if we want to keep our employment. I, for one, enjoy having enough food to eat, and the means to purchase material for a new apron now and then."

He seized her and pulled her against him. "Can I trust you? You're not like other girls. You do what you want, what moves your wild heart."

She put her arms around his neck. "My wild heart wants only you." When he tried to look away with an angry shrug, she brought his gaze back to hers. "Only you, Daniel."

He pressed his face against her neck then, in that way he had when his emotion was too strong to contain.

She stroked his hair. "Folk would gossip just the same if I stayed here alone with you. More in fact, because there wouldn't be anyone to say differently. I'll go and do this, and when we come back, I want us to marry. I've been thinking—I'm ready to go to Canada. We'll go and find a better life. We'll leave this place and never think of it again."

He held her tightly. "I love you," he said.

"I love you, Daniel."

The next day, the women left him standing on the pier and went with Aodhàn Mackinnon and his father to Mingulay.

AODHÀN ASSISTED LILITH OUT OF THE DINGHY AND ONTO DRY LAND, BUT he gave the same impersonal assistance to her mother and to Sarah. He steadied the boat while Euan Kilgore carried his father out then he was off, helping with the unloading of luggage.

The rest of the day was spent setting up the one house big enough and proper enough to accommodate them. Built of grey granite, it sat on the hill above the only village on Mingulay, looking down upon it and the riotous sea beyond. It had been abandoned at some point in time, and was now owned by the Catholic Church. Aodhàn had rented it for a month.

Lilith fell into bed exhausted after a day of cleaning, polishing, lugging kitchen supplies, cooking, and attending Kenneth Mackinnon, who suffered a severe coughing fit shortly after arriving. No one had told her she was to be his nurse as well as his companion on this sabbatical.

Sarah's snoring, and a mind that refused to stop reviewing the day, kept her awake. She stared out the narrow window at a single twinkling star, and compared Aodhàn to Daniel.

With Daniel, her heart would always be safe. Daniel would die to protect her. And, now that she'd lived seventeen years and had seen something of folk and what drove them, she knew he was right about Aodhàn. The factor's son, trapped on an obscure Hebridean isle with his ailing father, simply wanted to lessen the tedious march of time with a female, and Lilith was handy. If she succumbed to his charm, he would take what he wanted then disappear or, more likely, make her disappear.

Daniel was warm and comforting. She could picture a long future with him. They were from the same walk of life, and they fit each other seamlessly. Daniel would pledge himself to her and no other, for as long as they lived.

Aodhàn might be drawn to her for whatever reason, but their opposite stations formed an impenetrable wall between them. He'd always had servants to leap to his every desire. He'd never had to worry about where his next meal was coming from, or if he would have a home to live in.

I will not be one of those who leap to serve him, she thought. She would perform whatever tasks were required of her and keep to the background. It shouldn't be that hard to avoid Aodhàn. She would make certain she always had someone around—her mother, Sarah, or even Kenneth Mackinnon. The old man was scrupulously conventional.

It would be better if she didn't have this almost overwhelming physical attraction that ignited whenever Aodhàn came within eyesight. But it didn't matter. She was made of strong enough stuff to hold him off.

She quietly opened the drawer in the nightstand and brought out the necklace Aodhàn had given her so long ago. It captured the faint starlight from the window and quickly warmed against her skin. As much as she secretly treasured it, she had to give the necklace back.

After that, she would take every measure to avoid Aodhàn Mackinnon.

Mingulay

April,
1845

Chapter

Eleven

EUAN KILGORE WHEELED KENNETH MACKINNON UP THE HILL BEHIND their cottage and over to Bual na Creige, the blackest, highest, and most awe-inspiring of Mingulay's western cliffs, a savage sharp precipice that plunged straight down, hundreds upon hundreds of feet, to an unruly, unforgiving ocean.

Lilith sat on a blanket beside Kenneth's Bath chair, reading from *A Christmas Carol*, by Charles Dickens. The air was redolent with the stench of bird waste, and ringing with the shrill cries of thousands of seabirds. Almost lost beneath the noise came the bleating of new baby lambs, for April was lambing time on Mingulay.

Euan went off to explore the sheer vertical edge, leaving Lilith and Kenneth alone.

"'Sometimes people new to the business called Scrooge Scrooge, and sometimes Marley, but he answered to both names. It was all the same to him,'" Lilith read.

"I know what you're up to," Kenneth interrupted. "You think you can trick my son into marriage. I won't have it, do you understand?" He started coughing; Lilith jumped up and held a handkerchief to his mouth, but he pushed her away and took the cloth from her. He swiped at his lips, clenched his fist, and pounded the armrest. "I forbid it, do you hear me?"

"I'm not doing that," she said.

He cut her off with an angry wave and shook his index finger in her face. "You'll not ruin my son."

"I don't want your son," she shouted. "I'm already promised. I'm marrying Daniel, your groom."

He blinked, taken aback. "But Aodhàn said...."

His squint was openly suspicious. "You're marrying Daniel, you say?"

"Here's his ring." She pulled it out from under her collar.

There was a pause while he studied the ring and absorbed her statement. "Make sure you do and I'll provide a handsome dowry."

"I don't want your bribes, either!"

"But you will have the dowry, if you marry Daniel when we return. You know you'll need it, so don't be too quick to reject my offer. Daniel has told me he intends to move to Canada. I will fund your voyage and give you enough to support you for months—a year—when you get there."

She wanted to tell him to choke on his money, but she stopped herself, knowing very well how much something like that would help.

"You are not like other servant girls," he said, studying her. "Daft, silly, idiot creatures. You look at me like one of these birds." He waved vaguely at the cacophony before them. "Like an eagle." He nodded and punched the arm of the chair with his forefinger. "Fierce and unafraid. Will marriage to any man suit you? I wonder." He paused and started to turn away, muttering, "I can see…." He made a sharp gesture with one thin, pale hand. "Bah!"

That night, she stood in the corridor outside the parlor, eavesdropping. Aodhàn leaned on the fireplace mantel, one boot propped on the grate. She heard nothing untoward for a while. He and his father spoke of Mingulay, of the weather, of Barra and the crofters, of Oxford and the competitive infighting between the students, and of places they missed in Edinburgh.

Kenneth finally broached the subject she'd hoped for. "The chit Lilith has told me she is promised to Daniel Carson. She says they are soon to marry. So you see, your fine little romance with the scullery maid is all in your head."

Lilith saw Aodhàn's fingers whiten against his whisky glass. "I don't care what she said. Lilith is going to be my wife. You had better get used to it."

"I will cut you off without a penny to your name, boy!"

"No you won't."

"Don't test me!" Kenneth struggled to rise.

Aodhàn crossed to him, pushing him down. "Euan," he said. "The laudanum."

"I have it here, sir." Kenneth's man came forward with a bottle and a spoon.

"Listen to me," Kenneth said. "I forbid you to speak to that trollop. I'll send her back to Barra tomorrow. If you spoil my plans, I will get rid of her—permanently!" He was coughing badly now. Blood dribbled into his handkerchief and his voice hoarsened.

"Rest, Father," Aodhàn said. "You're making yourself ill. Everything will be just as you want it, I promise you."

That mollified the old man. "We'll find you an heiress," he rasped. Euan gave him a spoonful of medicine and bent so Kenneth could put his arms around his valet's neck. As Euan lifted him, he added, "We must do it quickly. I want to hold a grandchild before I die."

Lilith made her way upstairs before she could be discovered.

The next day, Kenneth kept to his bed and in the late afternoon Faith told Lilith she didn't need her for anything. "Go explore," she said. "See if you can find any trees besides that spindly one on the coast."

Lilith took care to make sure of Aodhàn's whereabouts first. After noting that he was writing at the desk in the parlor, she left, walking the other way so he wouldn't see her from the window.

She returned to the cliffs on the western side of the island, which drew her heart like a siren song. Wind was almost always blowing on Mingulay, and she loved that, too. Clouds were building. The air grew chill and blustery.

She crossed the frayed horsehair bridge over to Lianamuil, a high, sheered-off sea stack where crofters grazed their sheep. At the far edge she sat, dangling her legs over the edge, and pondered what she'd heard in the parlor. It threw all her carefully constructed opposition towards Aodhàn into disarray. He'd told his father he meant to marry her? That was not the action of a man seeking a meaningless physical dalliance with a servant.

She felt the restless tumbling of the sea, coupled with a demanding punch of wind against her face. A snow-white crescent moon rose as, on the opposite side of the sky, the sun descended. The music of it all coiled in her blood. She could no more ignore the call than she could stop her breathing. At first she merely swayed back and forth, but it wasn't enough. She had to stand, to dance there at the edge, dance for the moon. She entreated the spirits of the air to come out of the clouds and join her. She could almost see their faces, just beyond her reach, pale, cold, beautiful, drawing her onward, outward. Just as she reached beyond the safety of land and into empty space, she was gripped from behind and jerked backward.

Crying out in surprise, she swung around. "What are you doing?"

"Keeping you alive!" Aodhàn shouted.

She took in his terrified expression. His hands gripped her shoulders hard enough to leave bruises. He pulled her from the edge. Not until they stood near the center of the sea stack did he release her and swipe one trembling hand through his hair.

"I—I was only dancing," she said. But thinking back, she realized the voices of the sea and air had mesmerized her into leaning so far out she might not have been able to return.

He may have truly saved her life. He obviously thought so.

Straightening, he kept his eyes closed as he inhaled a long, deliberate breath and exhaled. He shook his arms as though trying to get the blood flowing before opening his eyes. "Are you cold?" He removed his coat and draped it over her shoulders.

"Surely you have better things to do than follow me about, sir," she said.

"No." He smiled briefly. "There is nothing better than this."

"Your father made it very clear what he thinks of me. Have you told him there's some romance between us?"

"Of course I have. You're going to be his daughter, and soon."

She released an angry sigh. "Christ Almighty. *Daniel's* going to be my husband."

His lips whitened. He grabbed her arms and shook her.

"Release me at once!" she cried.

"You will marry me, Lilith."

"I will never marry you. We both know what you want."

He stepped away, running a hand through his hair again. His jaw clenched. "I will marry you right now," he said. "We'll fetch the village priest."

She scoffed. "And send your father to an early grave."

"He won't die. He wants grandchildren too much."

"This is daft. Good night, Mr. Mackinnon."

"Let me walk you back."

She sighed, but made no argument. The wind had begun to bite and it was nearly dark. She smelled rain.

The rope bridge flapped violently. Lilith held tightly onto the rough handholds. The crossing went much more slowly than it had before and she was acutely aware that nothing more than woven horsehair kept her from plummeting into the roaring sea far below.

They went up the hill separating the cliffs from the rest of the island and as they descended the other side, she slipped on the grass. Aodhàn caught her arm and didn't let go. "Careful," he said. When they came to the rear of the cottage, his grip tightened and he pulled her under the eaves, behind a cascade of ivy. He brushed her windblown hair behind her ears and ran two fingertips over her cheek to her mouth. "Forgive me," he said. "I've been crude. Overbearing. I've never been patient. Give me another chance, Lilith."

"Another chance for what? I'm a servant. You're...not. I dust your furniture. That's as close as anything will ever get between us. I may not be rich or titled, but that doesn't mean I can be used as if I don't have any value."

His mouth worked, but he said, "If I swear I won't bring up the subject of marriage anymore, or touch you at all, will you allow me to show you a few of the most beautiful and hidden spots on the island?"

"Your father didn't bring me here to have a holiday." Why was she standing here talking to him? He wasn't holding onto her—she should leave immediately. Yet she lingered.

"What if I arrange for a chaperone?"

"A chaperone! Who has time for such things?"

"Your mother, if I say so."

"My mother would be the first to tell you she has better things to do."

"I've already asked her. She wants to go. Would you deny her an afternoon of pleasure?"

"No."

"Well, then. Tomorrow, if the weather is better?"

FAITH HAD VERY LITTLE TO SAY ABOUT THEIR OUTING, ONLY THAT THE DAY was pleasant, and that they should take along a basket of food. Aodhàn obligingly carried it and they descended to the village, where he arranged to have the use of a sailboat—for, he claimed, the west side of Mingulay was something to behold, and today the sea was calm enough to allow them to do so.

"Such rare conditions shouldn't be wasted," he said, smiling at them both as he put the basket into the dinghy that would transport them to the little sailboat anchored in the bay. He held out his hand to assist Faith, but she held back.

"Mam?" Lilith held out her hand too, so Faith would feel steadier. She'd always been oddly afraid of water.

"I know I'll get seasick," Faith said.

"Look how smooth and mild it is."

"Not enough for me. You go on. It's fine."

"I don't know." Lilith hadn't considered that her mother might change her mind about going. Uneasy, she said, "I'll go back with you."

"Not necessary." Faith didn't even glance at Aodhàn as she waved. "You'll enjoy it, you like those cliffs. You should see them from below. Go on."

Holding up the edge of her skirt, she started back towards the village.

"Lilith?" Aodhàn's tone was noncommittal.

She hesitated, but in the end, accepted Aodhàn's hand and climbed into the dinghy. Something told her he'd meant what he said about never forcing her, and she did want to look up at those cliffs.

The
Lamb

April,
1845

Chapter

Twelve

"YOU'VE BEEN HERE BEFORE?" LILITH ASKED.

Aodhàn glanced upward as they passed Lianamuil, this time from below. "I come here sometimes during holidays."

"Instead of going home?"

He met her gaze. "There are times I prefer to be alone." Nodding at the high cliffs on their left, he said, "I climbed these."

She snorted skeptically. "How?"

"Ropes, patience, skill—maybe a hint of madness. Folk have been climbing them for as long as they've had hands and feet."

The boat glided into ominous shadow. Aodhàn dropped the sail and took up the oars. Lilith held her bonnet to keep it from falling off as she craned her head backward.

They entered a keen-edged split, which Aodhàn told her was called Bagh na h-Aioneig—Bay of the Steep Promontory, and she had to admit his Gaelic was quite good. The air was chilly; the shrieking of countless birds bounced and echoed. It was an eerie place, the opaque black rock rising sheer above them, unimaginably high, like the implacable torso of a colossal ancient god. Lilith imagined him gazing down upon them with the austere remote indifference born of ageless-ness and invincibility.

She stared at the far off summit. "I stood there," she said, half-disbelievingly.

"Aye." He rowed out of the shadow and guided the boat south-wards; strong southbound currents carried them swiftly along. "There's a cave I want to show you," he said. They passed more cliffs, some with great hollowed out caves, and he rowed them through a dark tunnel with an arched roof, like the ceiling in a cathedral but for the bird shit that whitened everything.

The cave he sought came into view. As he steered them towards it, Lilith heard, below the sound of waves washing against stone, a faint, anxious bleat. She rose onto her knees, gripping the side of the boat, and saw, not far from them, a soaked, limp, wad of fluff—a lamb in the water.

"Oh," she cried. "Aodhàn! Go closer, go closer!" She only realized she'd called him by his Christian name as he obediently sliced the water with an oar, veering them towards the animal.

She reached over the side and plucked out the lamb. It released another pitiful sound, along with a trail of watery blood from the corner of its mouth.

"Oh, God," she whispered, cradling it. It was mortally wounded—she sensed there would be no hope of rescue here.

"It must have fallen," Aodhàn said. He rowed them to the cave and with one strong swipe of the oars, pushed the prow up onto a shelf of sand. Leaping out, he dragged the boat farther and when it was secure, held Lilith's elbow and her waist, steadying her as she climbed out, still cradling the lamb in her arms like a baby.

She hardly even glanced at the surroundings. It was an unremark-able cave, shaped like a half-moon, with a sand, rock, and shingle floor. A cairn of sea-smoothed rocks sat near the back, where, perhaps, it escaped being swamped at high tide. She dropped to the sand, murmuring to the injured lamb. It was hard to tell what had happened when it fell. The collision with the water from so high up had probably injured it inside. It grew weaker by the moment; if she hadn't supported its head, it would have dangled almost lifelessly. Its eyes opened and closed, more and more slowly. She could only hold it, speak to it, stroke it, and weep over it, hoping to ease its passing.

Aodhàn sat beside her and stroked the lamb as well. She glanced at him and was surprised to see a sorrowful expression.

"I wonder how often this happens," he said.

She brushed at her eyes. A few moments passed and the lamb stopped breathing, which was a relief—at least it no longer suffered.

Aodhàn put his hand on her forearm, then her shoulder. She looked up to his face, blurry through her tears, but the anguish was clear. It softened her; impulsively she rested her palm against his cheek. The warmth of his skin startled her and she quickly withdrew, embarrassed.

He took the lamb, and when she started to rise, pushed her gently down again. "I'll do what's necessary," he said.

Using one of the oars, he dug a grave at the very back. As he picked up the corpse to place it in the hole she turned away, not wanting to see, and allowed the movement, the light and shadow, the whisper of the sea, to take over her mind.

He came back, dropped, and put his arm around her.

She knew she shouldn't allow such liberties, but he kept the embrace impersonal, the same sort of comfort a stranger might offer. She felt so heartsick she ignored her internal warnings and rested her cheek against his shoulder.

They sat that way for a long time, as sunlight traced across the water.

"I've watched the sea every day of my life, but it's never right," she said. "It's not the right color. It doesn't smell right. When I close my eyes, the sea in my mind is blue and green, shot with light, water you can see through, not this heavy dark wall. The sea in my mind is made of rainbows; even though I dive deep, it allows me to breathe, and it's warm—not like this sea."

His arm tightened.

"I've always felt I'm in the wrong place, the wrong time."

"There is no right place for you and me anymore," Aodhàn said. "We're adrift, aimless, with no answers, no path to follow. I don't know if there is a purpose anymore, or if we are cursed to do this without end, for as long as the sun rises and sets."

Though his answer made little sense, Lilith felt he understood what she was trying to say.

If only it wouldn't wound Daniel, she would like to spend more time with this man.

The tide rose. Heavy swells crashed against the cliffs. They climbed back into the boat and Aodhàn rowed them away from the dark, immutable cliffs and sad cave, out into bright sunlight. Lilith watched the slight mound at the back of the cave for as long as she could, and whispered, "Rest well," as it fell out of sight. Poor wee thing, all alone, with only one, maybe two, humans to mourn it. And its mother, who would search and never know what happened.

Open sea brought a helpful wind; the sails filled and carried them around the southern tip of the island. From there it was only a few strokes with the oars to get them back to the bay beside the village.

"Time for our picnic," Aodhàn said, after he'd tied the sailboat to its buoy and helped her into the dinghy.

She hadn't realized how hungry she was until he mentioned food.

"It seems only right to eat it," he said. "Since your mother went to the trouble. Shall we go up on the hill there? Càrnan, it's called. The day is so clear, I think we can see Barra, and over to the lighthouse on Berneray as well."

"Aye," she said. "If you like."

They passed the cottage on the way up. Sarah, hanging wet bed sheets out to dry, waved then stood and watched them, hands on hips.

Perhaps she wondered what had happened to their chaperone, and was arguing with herself over what she should do about it. In the end, she went back inside.

There was a bottle of wine in the basket, a joint of mutton, cheese, and new-baked bread. There was even a covered dish of pretty little mince pies sprinkled with sugar.

An almost cloudless sky did make it possible to see the humps of every island to the north, and over to the imposing cliffs of Berneray, with its gleaming lighthouse.

The wind was just right, a breeze that cooled them from their climb. Puffins and gulls came over to visit and beg. They put on quite a show, which gradually lightened Lilith's mood and brought her to laughter once or twice.

She would remember the lamb though, and think of it. It was all she could do.

Aodhàn took her by surprise when he kissed her hand.

"No—don't," she said, pulling free.

He frowned. "I thought we were past all that."

"We can never be. It's impossible."

"You're forcing yourself to be like every other insipid female I've ever known. I hate it! Admit the truth. You know you want to be with me."

She sighed impatiently. He was only half right. She didn't want to be with him as much as she wanted to honor her word to Daniel.

She got up and walked away to the edge of land. He followed and again grabbed her hand. This time, she didn't pull free, since he merely put himself between her and the cliff.

The Atlantic swelled and glittered in the sunlight. The wind changed, buffeting them from the west.

An eagle circled, watching.

"I'll build you a summer house here," he said, "since you love it so much."

She shook her head, torn between laughter and irritation. "I'm not a prostitute, sir. How many times must I explain that to you?"

He pulled her to a stop and faced her, holding her cheeks. "You will marry me, Lilith." His frown was a fearsome thing.

"Why do you keep talking this way? I'm nobody. Your da—"

"Is a factor, and I'm a factor's son. That's all." The wind picked up his hair and blew it wildly. "Shall we force his hand? If your belly has his grandson in it, he'll agree. I know him."

He leaned in again, his eyes hungry.

"I'm going to marry Daniel," she reminded him, though softly, to lessen the sting. She realized she cared more now about his feelings. The day they'd spent together had changed her.

His mouth thinned, betraying his anger. He straightened. "Go ahead," he shouted. "Marry him. Give up everything I'm offering you. Bear a whelp every year who never stops howling and sucks you dry."

He stalked away.

She wanted to tell him she didn't mean to hurt him, and that she was sorry. But she gritted her teeth and let him go.

Greyson's Orders

April,
1845

Chapter

Thirteen

A MENACING RUMBLE OF THUNDER SPLIT THE HEAVENS AND VIBRATED through the boat rail under Aodhàn's hands as Lilith and Faith hurried away from the pier at Castlebay. The rain, which had thankfully held off during their tumultuous voyage back to Barra, unleashed all at once with stinging ferocity.

The torrent immediately swallowed the two women behind a murky curtain.

When the messenger brought news of Daniel's worsening illness, Lilith had insisted on going back. Faith had agreed and Aodhàn decided to escort them, leaving Sarah, Euan, and Kenneth on Mingulay.

The wind intensified long before they reached Barra. Lilith and Faith had to bend over and hold their bonnets on their heads as they raced off to their cottage.

Sheets of hail joined the rain as Aodhàn struggled towards Bishop House. Within moments, a layer of ice slicked the ground as far as he could see. He was shivering by the time he reached the manor house, and glad to find a fire in the drawing room.

Greyson came forward and helped Aodhàn remove his sodden coat. "I was afraid you would come back as soon as you received my message," he said. "I'm relieved you made it safely, my lord. Are storms like this routine here?"

"You would know better than I," Aodhàn said roughly. "I'm freezing."

"Come stand by the fire. I'll ring for tea."

The local woman left to cook and care for the house while the family was gone brought a tray. Greyson poured and Aodhàn soon began to feel warmer. When they were alone, he said, "Well? Tell me. What's happened? Did you do as I asked?"

"Yes, my lord." Greyson sighed deeply and studied the fire. A lump of coal dropped out through the grate. He swept it up and slid it back in. "He died a few hours ago."

"He's dead? The messenger said he was ill."

"Yes, when I sent notice, he was alive. Barely."

A fresh shiver, caused by something colder than the weather, ran through him.

Daniel was dead.

The king of Idómeneus's beloved bastard son. A handsome boy, until the lioness got hold of him.

Aodhàn swiveled, certain someone had come in the room, but there was no one. No one but Greyson, who remained by the fireplace, his shoulders slumped. Yet the feeling of being watched persisted. He went to the doorway and looked both ways. The corridor was empty.

"How did you do it?" he asked after coming back.

"Arsenic," Greyson said, so low Aodhàn almost didn't hear him. "They will think it cholera—I hope."

"How? How did you—what did you—did he drink it? Eat it?"

"Cora, the girl who brought your tea just now? She has been feeding Daniel as well as me, since he came every day to care for the horses. I mixed it in his porridge."

Greyson studied him, his expression morose, almost accusing.

There had been no other way. Lilith's loyalty would never allow her to succumb to Aodhàn's advances, no matter how much she wanted to. Once upon a time, Queen Aridela of Crete had carried more loyalty in a single strand of hair than any man he knew, and in the end, that loyalty had been her doom.

She might look different and sound different now, but Aridela lived on inside Lilith, influencing her in ways she couldn't imagine.

Only he suffered the raw, unfiltered memories of every life—Alexiare as well, though the old man had to have his memories forced back in. Now, as Aodhàn sat in the drawing room hearing the news of Daniel's death, he realized he was free to pursue and win her, the only woman he could ever want, the woman he had just killed for. He shivered yet again.

He saw the fear and regret in Greyson's eyes. Poor old Alexiare. The two men stared at each other. Aodhàn thought he heard a cry, like an eagle on the hunt.

The faint sound promised a reckoning. It brought back, vividly, the things that had been done to him in other lives.

At that moment, he would have given anything to go back, to reverse his demand, to find another way.

But it was too late.

SOMEONE POUNDED ON THE FRONT DOOR. CORA, DRYING HER HANDS ON A towel, ran from the kitchen to open it. The commotion brought Aodhàn and Greyson out of the parlor.

It was Faith and one of the local men. Both were wet through. Faith looked miserable, blue with cold.

"Come in," Aodhàn said, and closed the door behind them, shutting out the wind and rain.

"Is she here?" Faith asked, not bothering with greetings. Water ran over her face. Even her voice trembled.

"She? Who?" Aodhàn guided them both into the warm parlor.

"The girl. Lilith," the local man said.

"No." Aodhàn's earlier unease intensified into fear. "Isn't she with you?"

Faith shook her head. "Peter Bateson was waiting for us at the cottage. Daniel is dead. Lilith—when Lilith saw him, she...she—"

The man she'd come with put his arm around her shoulders, but she shrugged him off.

"She ran out," he said. "Screamed and ran out. My sons and I have been searching, and a few others, but she's just...gone. We thought she might have come here."

Aodhàn felt dizzy and faint, as though all the blood had drained from his head. Lilith, out, alone, in this? Greyson put a steadying hand on his arm and drew him away.

"My lord," he whispered next to Aodhàn's ear, "I've been watching her a long time. I know the places she goes."

Aodhàn followed him into the corridor. As he thrust his arms into the sleeves of a dry coat, Greyson shared what he knew.

Faith and the others were still talking as Aodhàn slipped out through the kitchen.

SHE STOOD AS STILL AS A STANDING STONE. BUT FOR THE FLASH OF lightning, Aodhàn never would have seen her at all. Shouting, "Lilith!"

he ran through the downpour to her side. Another lightning bolt illuminated her face. Her lips were dark, her eyes no more than black shadows.

He grabbed her, since she never even glanced at him. He shook her, but she went on staring at the sea. He heard the waves crashing demonically.

She hadn't thrown herself in.

For the first time, he realized that's what he'd expected. He'd thought that would be his punishment. But she was here, alive. He nearly sobbed in relief.

He opened his coat and wrapped it around her as far as it would go. "Lilith," he whispered.

She didn't respond. Her silence and stillness reminded him of a mortally wounded animal.

"We must get you warm." He pulled her away from the bluff, back to Bishop House.

THE WINDOWS WERE ILLUMINATED AND THE FRONT DOOR WIDE OPEN. Aodhàn saw men and women crowded in the foyer. One look and Aodhàn knew he would not take her in there, no matter how troubled her mother was, or anyone else for that matter. He couldn't subject her to that. He pressed her icy cold face against his shoulder.

Bypassing the house, he guided her to the stables. It would be dry in there, at least.

He lit a lantern and led her to an empty stall. There he stripped off her coat, tossing it into the corner, then her sodden dress and corset. He rubbed her arms, her shoulders. He knelt and rubbed her legs.

Through it all, she simply stared, frowning. The anguish in her expression tore at him. He'd done this; by doing it, had he lost any chance of having her, ever, in this life? What if she never recovered?

He rose. "Lilith? Lilith?" He held her cheeks in his hands. She was still so horribly cold.

Suddenly, she blinked. Her eyes narrowed. She saw him.

"Aodhàn," she whispered. She looked to the right, then to the left. "The stables."

He realized then what a terrible mistake he'd made, bringing her here, to Daniel's domain.

She put her hand to her throat. Her gaze rose to his again. Her eyes were wide and black. Catching her lower lip under her teeth, she lifted her hand and touched his mouth. A low, sobbing moan slipped from her.

Then she kissed him. She pressed against him, hard, seizing the back of his head then grabbing fistfuls of his hair with both hands, as though afraid he would shy away.

But he would never do that. Not even when he should.

Chapter

Fourteen

SHE CAME UP THROUGH A THOUSAND FATHOMS OF WATER TO A WARM scent, the rustle of straw, and horses nickering.

Where was she?

With a sigh she sat up, rubbing her eyes.

The storm had blown itself out, or away. Sunlight crept through cracks in the walls, making dust particles glitter like flurries of miniature stars. She was lying on a thick, soft pile of straw.

Daniel's stables.

Daniel.

She'd torn the blanket off him. She'd called Peter Bateson a wicked liar.

But Daniel didn't respond to her entreaties. He didn't take her hand. He didn't do anything but lie there, colorless. His eyes remained closed. He refused to come back to her, even though she begged.

"Daniel," she whispered. Saying it sucked the air clear out of her lungs. She pressed her face against her knees. "My Daniel."

Aodhàn half woke and pulled her in, caressing her shoulder.

She closed her eyes and imagined it was Daniel's hand. It felt like putting something cold and numbing on a hot, throbbing tooth.

"Lilith," Aodhàn said softly.

She kept her eyes closed. "Thank you," she said. "I—I'm sorry."

"You're apologizing?"

"I wanted Daniel."

He paused, then said, "I know." He stroked her hair. "I hope I didn't hurt you."

She was sore. But she shook her head and put her face against his neck. He was warm, his pulse steady, comforting. They lay in a rustling cocoon, where she could pretend nothing had happened. That it had been a dream.

101

Wait—there had been a dream. She'd dreamed of Daniel. Of his voice, anyway.

I will wait for you.

Before she could examine the dream, perhaps expand on it, there was a crash. The big stable door bounced off the wall, letting in a flood of bright light.

Both of them jerked. Aodhàn put himself between Lilith and the two men staring at them.

"S-sir?" one said. "Is that—is that the missing girl? Lilith Kelso?"

Aodhàn jumped to his feet. "Get out of here!" he shouted.

They did, quickly.

Lilith found her corset and dress, but both were still as wet as when Aodhàn had removed them.

"Wait here," he said, pulling on his wet trousers. "I'll fetch you something dry. You're moving into Bishop House, Lilith. Today."

Acceptance

August,
1845

Chapter

Fifteen

For the next month, the residents of Barra suffered blind terror at every rising mist. Rumor claimed a sickly fog had enveloped Faith's cottage the day before Daniel fell ill, and when no one else succumbed, the church reverberated with prayers of thanks.

While many praised Aodhàn Mackinnon for bringing Faith and Lilith into Bishop House to protect them from the miasma, a simultaneous undercurrent of something else traveled with greater speed across the island.

Peter and Gavin caught them together—naked.

Do you think Aodhàn Mackinnon killed Daniel?

It was miasma, wasn't it?

Awfully nice timing. The same day the factor's son returned from a month-long holiday...with her.

What about her? Lying with another man the same day Daniel died...and they were betrothed!

She's odd. Always has been. Never cared about folk at all.

I knew she would end up a whore. It was there in those eyes—as cold as a wolf's. I saw it. There's no Christian modesty in that chit. Nor a soul, I'd wager.

The talk veered then into how Lilith never attended church, and how God caused Daniel to die as a punishment, since he never went either.

But she and Faith had the powerful protection of the factor, so the gossip was quiet, and studiously kept from the ears of those who worked in the big house.

A baby boy was born to one of the village women. Aodhàn ordered a basket of food and other appropriate gifts sent to the family.

Could it be Menoetius? He would wonder every time a child was born for the rest of his life, no doubt. As the keeper of the memories, he'd learned that Goddess Athene's chosen triad wasn't always reborn right away. For instance, the first time he saw Lilith, the day she and Daniel dropped out of the hole in his bedroom wall, the memories of all their lives returned in a sickening flood and he realized that centuries had passed since the last time he'd seen her. The world was very different.

Sometimes he marveled at the way humans clung to old and tired traditions. Other times he hardly recognized anything, so great were the changes.

Menoetius could be reborn within hours of his death...or it might be hundreds of years. Only the bitch goddess knew.

He studied the infant as it was baptized, but saw nothing out of the ordinary. He would not be able to tell anyway, not until it grew old enough for the tingling and aura to develop.

As time passed and Daniel's death appeared to be forgotten in favor of more immediate concerns, like the odd reduction in the usually massive schools of herring so many Barra fishermen relied upon, he breathed more easily, and allowed himself to hope.

Lilith resisted him. She withdrew after their night of passion, and refused to lie with him again. He knew why she'd done it; it wasn't for love or even attraction that she had given him her body. Her grief had been too agonizing to bear. She had used him as a lifeline, a means to survive the next few moments. The only victory he could award himself was that he'd managed to distract her for hours.

He'd known her motive and he hadn't challenged it, but now, after four months, he felt as though a thousand stickpins were piercing him every instant of the day and night. He wanted her. Needed her. He had to do something, and soon. He'd taken drastic measures to open the way—now he wanted things to happen quickly. He was tired of waiting, and deep inside, he constantly feared punishment.

Waking one morning in late August, his need so intense he wasn't certain he could bear it another day, he went to the kitchen in search of her.

Faith was kneading bread dough. "She's out on the bluffs. She goes out every morning and stands by the water. I think if I didn't allow her to do that, she would fade away and vanish. She talks to Daniel out there." She sent him a dark, accusing glance. "You need to do something. You're losing her. I'm losing her. You told me you intend to make her your wife. Well, there's no Daniel in your way now. What are you waiting for?"

"What d'you want me to do? I can't force her to marry me."

"If you got her pregnant, she would."

"Are you telling me to rape her?"

"If that's what it takes. I want to see her get on with life. This mourning is beyond normal."

Faith was a cold woman, no doubt about it. Yet she would term it mere practicality. There was worry under her blunt words.

He went off to the hills, not knowing what he would do.

Chapter

Sixteen

LILITH LAY ON HER BACK, SURROUNDED BY WILDFLOWERS. EYES CLOSED against the sunlight, she listened to the wash of the tide and remembered the first time she ever saw Daniel.

She'd been playing with the kit. Something had sent her body tingling, like she'd swallowed live sparks. She'd looked up and had seen the silhouettes of Daniel and her mother coming towards her from the direction of the sea. The colors around him had been intense in those first moments, with the sunlight behind him. She remembered blinking, thinking there was something wrong with her eyes, but no. His figure had been outlined in a dark blue halo.

She had believed him a creature from the sea. Her mam had brought him home to be her playmate.

At first he'd been hurt, like the kit. But she healed him. Gradually, his eyes lost that sea-shimmer. He became a real human boy.

That very morning, the morning Faith brought him, Lilith had sung to the sea, asking for a companion. No—she'd asked for her twin. She was lonely around these people she couldn't understand. They bellowed and smelled. They grated on her ears and mind. She longed for silence so she could hear the sea's voice and feel the sea's embrace.

She knew she was half of a whole. She asked the sea to either take her back, or bring her twin to keep her company.

Not an hour after, Daniel appeared.

"*What did it mean when I lost the soft hills,*" she sang under her breath. "*Time melts into mine, jewels and ancient forgiveness.*"

She didn't know if she'd made up the lyrics herself when she was little, or if she'd heard them somewhere. The words were a magic spell. They spoke of the past and the future, too, of something that would happen someday.

After they knew each other better, Daniel confided that he'd come from a land beneath the sea, a palace made of pearl and silver, gold and shell. He told her that's where he lived while he waited for her.

"For me?"

He'd nodded. "I'm a prince there. But I always want to come back to you. I'm miserable until she allows me to be with you."

"She?"

"The queen of that place. My mother." He'd touched the red, scabbed-over wound at the side of his left eye. "She marks me before I leave, so I won't forget her." The wound had healed, but left a crescent shaped scar that severed his brow, curving outward then back in, coming to a final sharp point halfway down his cheekbone.

From the moment she'd first looked into his eyes, Daniel made her feel complete.

As they grew older, he stopped talking about the palace beneath the sea. Years later, when she reminded him of it, he scoffed and said it was never real, it was just a story he'd invented, a way to endure the grief of his mother's death. When she'd pointed at his scar as proof, he said the scar was from one of many thrashings his da had given him.

She opened her hand and looked at Aodhàn's ornament, sparkling in the sunlight.

The necklace was crafted in a legendary pool, a secret cavern where the moon went into hiding when it disappeared from the skies. Though the queen is long dead, her great civilization lost, the necklace goes on casting her spell, century after century, for within it is forged the amaranthine light of the moon.

Aodhàn spoke to her soul in different ways. He, too, made her feel complete. It frightened her, how he induced the same need, the same consummation, as Daniel did.

Yet it also felt right.

"Lilith?"

The grass rustled in her ear as she twisted her head.

Time melts into mine.

Aodhàn stood over her, looking down tenderly.

"I've been thinking about the story you told me," she said.

He dropped down beside her, crossing his legs. "What story?"

"The queen and her necklace. I feel like I know her. I dream of her. She has black hair. There are rivers of fire. There's a man—a man like a lion."

She was holding the necklace by its chain, watching it rotate in the breeze. When he said nothing, she looked at him and was shocked to see tears in his eyes. He turned his head away, like he hoped she wouldn't see.

"Aodhàn?" She put her hand on his chest. The pendant bounced against him then fell into the grass.

For the first time she saw him as a man rather than Aodhàn Mackinnon, the remote and haughty factor's son.

"I never see those colors around you anymore," she said, wanting to distract him from whatever had saddened him. "But for an instant, in the stables that night, after the lantern went out."

"It fades when it's no longer needed."

She wondered what that meant, but followed another thought. "I still feel the lightning though. When we touch. It shocks, like in winter, when you walk barefoot across a rug then touch a blanket. But it lasts longer."

He nodded and smiled, his eyes still misty, his black feathery lashes clumped. "That's the magic between us. That's why you were drawn to me from the moment you met me. It's why you gave yourself to me when you were grieving. See?" He placed his index finger on her cheek and a slight, trembling spark radiated into her blood.

"I can make it stronger," he said, his eyes darkening. His other fingers joined the first. They stroked over her cheek and down to the pulse in her throat. Her entire body lit up in a fiery shiver.

"Say my name," he whispered.

"Why?"

"Because I like what your mouth does when you say it."

"What does it do?"

"It looks like you're wanting to kiss me."

"Aodhàn."

"See? Ooo-ghan."

"Aodhàn...."

He bent and kissed her. The fierceness of it said *I have waited long enough.* Lilith succumbed like a log burning to cinders.

When he lifted his face, she said, "I think I'd best only use your name when we're alone."

He smiled.

She knew then that she would marry him.

Evie

August,
1849

Chapter

Seventeen

"'ARE YOU POSSESSED WITH A DEVIL," HE PURSUED, SAVAGELY, "TO TALK IN that manner to me when you are dying? Do you reflect that all those words will be branded in my memory, and eating deeper eternally after you have left me? You know you lie to say I have killed you, and, Catherine, you know that I could as soon forget you as my existence! Is it not sufficient for your infernal selfishness, that while you are at peace I shall writhe in the torments of hell?'"

Lilith scooped a whining Claire into her arms. "Poor Heathcliff," she said. "Stir the soup, my wee love," she added.

Lilith knew how to distract her three-year-old from angst. The child giggled as she manhandled the spoon, trying to mimic what she'd seen her mam do.

"Aye." Aodhàn closed the book and sent Lilith an accusing stare. "You women make us mad with your flighty moods—one moment asking for kisses, the next eyeing younger, richer men."

"Poor Mackinnon." Lilith lifted her brows. "Or should I say Aodhàn? I wouldn't mind a kiss."

He rose immediately to comply. Lilith put Claire down and prepared to ladle the soup, scarcely more than a thin broth, into bowls. "Have you met the author? I swear he used you as his inspiration, for you are the full and complete incarnation of the devilish Heathcliff."

Aodhàn replied with wicked dark laughter.

"Go and fetch Greyson and your grandmam," Lilith said to Claire.

Their brief light mood dissipated as they sat down to eat. Lilith knew before they finished there would be scratching on the kitchen door, folk begging for scraps.

She always gave, and generously, though their own food supplies hardly surpassed the villagers', but it was just another reason to hate her.

There were some who blamed Lilith Kelso and Aodhàn Mackinnon entirely for the potato blight. More than a few believed God brought it as punishment for allowing their sin—no matter that the rot had spread to all the islands, and the mainland, and had already devastated Ireland.

Lilith wondered if God would really punish so many for the sins of two—and if he would, what did that say about him?

The same month the potatoes on Barra first putrefied, Lilith gave birth to a daughter. She named the child Claire, after Daniel's mother.

Lilith knew many of Barra's inhabitants didn't see this birth and the destruction of their main food crop as a coincidence. Nor did they appreciate the obvious happiness of the couple in the fine manor house when so many others suffered, or how one of their own, an undeserving one at that, had managed to rise out of her assigned station in life. She knew what they all believed she'd done to win the heart of John Gordon's factor.

Kenneth Mackinnon got his wish to hold a grandchild, but not for long. He'd died two months after Claire was born. One of Lilith's fondest memories was of the day he clasped her hand and said, "You are a good match for him. A good match."

Aodhàn took over as factor of Barra just in time to see the first of the worsening hunger and later, starvation, as everything seemed to align against the people. Even the herring vanished, and fishermen came home with half-empty nets. The bays were stripped of dulse, cockles, and anything else that could be eaten. Aodhàn wrote letter after letter to John Gordon, the island's owner, but to say the man was parsimonious was too kind. It wasn't until two died for lack of food and the government intervened that the man sent supplies and money for relief, and cancelled the overdue rents. It took many more desperate entreaties before he reluctantly paid for a hundred and fifty starving Barra residents to relocate to Glasgow, and added an offer to fund their further relocation to the Americas.

Of course, the remaining villagers decided Aodhàn was lying about the letters. Many accused him of sitting in his comfortable house waiting for them all to die, never mind that he would then be unemployed.

"Mackinnon," Lilith said suddenly. Her eyes opened wide.

"Aye?"

"I—I think I—"

Aodhàn rose so swiftly his chair fell over backwards. "Is it time, then?"

"Must be," she said, and pressed both hands to her swollen stomach.

Claire's eyes grew big and round. Greyson rose, saying, "Is there aught I can do?"

"Boil water," Aodhàn said. He picked Lilith up, ignoring her protests, and carried her out of the kitchen. Faith stood and followed, pausing on the way upstairs to collect a stack of linens.

Lilith labored all through the night. As the sky lightened in the morning, Faith announced she could see the coming baby's head.

Aodhàn took Lilith's hand. "Push hard now," he said, and within ten minutes, they had themselves another girl.

Faith held the baby up and slapped it on the rump so it would cry.

Claire climbed onto her father's lap, grinning hugely when told she had a sister. All through the pregnancy she'd said she wanted no smelly boy, and shouted *No!* whenever she was told she might have to accept one.

"She hurt!" Claire wailed upon seeing the wee wean.

"No," said Aodhàn. "She just needs a bathing, then she'll be pink and clean. Now give your mama a kiss. She worked aye hard to bring you your sister."

Lilith did her best to smile at her daughter, but she was so exhausted that as soon as her mother had her wiped and dry, she drifted off to sleep.

FAITH AND AODHÀN TOOK CLAIRE AND THE BABY TO THE KITCHEN SO Lilith could sleep in peace.

Faith made tea and Aodhàn held his new daughter. Not at all sleepy, Claire sat on his lap as well, peering over the edge of the blanket. Aodhàn absently smoothed her tangled hair. It was so fine it caused endless shrieking every morning when Lilith tried to brush it.

"I received a letter from the Colonel yesterday," he said.

"Aye?" Faith's expression didn't change. She knew better than to hope by now.

"He says if they won't pay their rents, he wants to send more of them away. Told me to make preparations, to charter a ship."

"Like as not away to die."

"Don't tell Lilith. I don't want her fretting."

"D'you truly believe you can hide this from her?"

The inevitable scratching interrupted them before he could answer.

"Please sir," said the woman at the door. "My baby is near death." She did indeed hold an infant, and it did look awful, too weak to even cry, as did the mother, who told them her husband was dead.

Aodhàn brought them in and sat them at the table. He left them to Faith while he took the children away, Claire to her bed and the new one to her mother, for she was beginning to make soft, wambly sounds of hunger.

Lilith rubbed her eyes. She held out her arms for the baby. "What shall we name her? I picked Claire's name. You choose."

He paused a long time. "What do you think of Evangeline?"

"'Tis a mouthful!" she said, smiling.

"She's a Mackinnon. Fortune favors the bold."

"Can we call her Evie?"

"Aye. Evie," he said, and kissed them both.

Barra

is

Purged

August,
1851

Chapter

Eighteen

LILITH WAS AWAKE WHEN AODHÀN SLIPPED OUT OF BED, BUT SHE pretended to sleep on. He moved carefully, in near silence, and soon left their bedroom to creep down the stairs. Only then did she get up and go to the window, where she could look upon the stables.

Two men were waiting for him. One of them held a lantern, the other the reins of an extra horse. With hardly any words exchanged, all three rode away into the darkness.

Though Aodhàn tried to keep it from her, she'd always known what was happening on Barra. It couldn't be hidden—not when so many folk were abandoning their homes in hopes of finding better lives elsewhere, or were coerced into leaving.

Though he was only twenty-five, grey had begun to thread through Aodhàn's black hair, and his nature, over the last five years, had gradually transformed from cheerful confidence to taciturn brooding. One evening, after Lilith handed out the last of their bread to a beggar, he said he would pack them up and leave, except he knew he was the only voice these people had with Colonel Gordon.

Today was the date set for a mandatory meeting between the Barra crofters and Colonel Gordon, to be held at nearby Lochboisdale, on Uist. On Gordon's orders, Aodhàn had relayed to the people that they would be fined if they didn't attend. He hadn't revealed this to Lilith, but she knew. Even though most never gossiped around her, she still managed to hear things, and little else had been talked about for weeks.

She dressed, collected her two daughters, and went down to the kitchen to make gruel. The girls were subdued. Perhaps their father's mood of late had rubbed off on them.

Faith was already there. They sat together at the table having tea.

"There are some who won't go to the meeting," Faith said.

"And some will refuse to pay a fine. What will the Colonel do to them?"

Faith shrugged.

"Why has this happened? We were never rich, but Barra provided. Now all has turned against us."

"More than a few say you are the cause."

"I know. I'm the devil incarnate. They don't care that you never go to church, but it's different when it comes to me. Why did you stop?"

"Because I knew it for what it was. Tripe."

Lilith smiled. She'd learned to be plain-spoken from Faith. It was too late by now to change either of them. "Men in fancy robes, seeking power."

After a pause, Faith said, "You should probably go, though."

"Why? I don't care what they think of me."

"You've weans to consider. And…there is more hatred towards you than you may realize."

Lilith understood her mother was warning her. "Is it something else besides not attending Mass or confession? Something other than marrying the cursed outsider?"

Faith sipped her tea. She glanced at the girls, who were playing in the corner with wooden animals Aodhàn had carved for them. Two-year-old Evie came over to Lilith and crawled onto her lap with an elephant, her favorite of the toy beasts. She loved to talk and did so almost constantly, unlike her mother at the same age. Lilith was the only one who understood it, though.

"Do you want to go to the bay and search for cockles?" she asked the child.

"Aye." Evie nodded.

"Just be careful," Faith said.

Frantic pounding on the front portal at Bishop House brought both Faith and Lilith from their laundry.

Two dirty women stood there, dressed in rags. "Our men are being attacked!" one cried, supporting the other. "Up at Balnabodach!"

"Who is attacking them?" Lilith asked.

"'Tis your husband, and the Sheriff, and his hired men!"

"Our children as well," the other said. "All are being beaten. Dragged away!"

Her gaze, landing upon Lilith, was black with fury.

"Watch the girls," Lilith said to Faith.

"What are you thinking of doing?"

"Mackinnon isn't beating anyone. I will go and see what's really going on." She gave the woman a glare of her own.

"Mam! Mam!" Evie clutched her skirts and refused to let go. She took the child, in the end, unable to leave her so upset.

When she had a mare saddled, she tucked Evie in front of her and whipped the animal, sending it at a gallop to Balnabodach.

LEAPING OFF HER HORSE ON THE SUMMIT OF A HILL ABOVE THE LOCH, Lilith held her daughter and stared, aghast, at madness.

Men, women, and children ran in every direction, screaming, shouting, fighting with armed soldiers. But they were sadly outnumbered, and even the men could hardly fight back in their weakened states. She watched one heavily armed mercenary sweep up a screaming toddler and toss him carelessly to one of his companions.

Where was Aodhàn? Who was doing this? Was all this simply to collect a few fines? She could see nothing then, and blinked furiously, realizing she was sobbing.

She started to put Evie down so she could go and join the fight, but Evie screamed and clamped like a limpet to her neck.

All she could do was stand, watch, and weep.

Then she saw Aodhàn. He *was* there. Those two he'd ridden off with earlier were with him. Aodhàn was shouting, but she couldn't hear his words. One of the men was shouting back. They came to blows, and the third man separated them.

A number of the brigands were busy destroying the crofters' homes, pulling off the thatch, breaking the walls with pickaxes and heavy tools, setting fire to anything that would burn. They used truncheons on those who fought. Aodhàn ran forward and pushed between one of the crofters and an armed recruit, taking several blows on his head before the soldier realized who he was.

It was almost over now. Most of the people had been herded into a group and led away. Lilith watched her husband arguing again with the two men. He gestured and swiped at the blood on his face, his demeanor clearly furious. Had he lost control over the soldiers? She couldn't tell.

He looked up and saw her on the hill, watching. He stared at her for a long moment. Then he spun away, and she felt his despair like a knife through her stomach.

A
Stranger
Comes
to
Barra

June,
1853

Chapter

Nineteen

NO MATTER WHAT NAMES HE INVENTED WHILE HIDING IN OTHER BODIES, the rough-looking man who paused on Castlebay's pier to study his surroundings would always think of himself as Harpalycus of Tiryns, son of a powerful king.

In those days, he was a well-made man, his muscles defined and strong from training with heavy shields and swords. He had women and slaves in plenty, and was heir to a mighty throne.

But just now he had to become the easily forgettable Owen Anderson, a common, dull lout somewhere in his forties, from a nameless village on the mainland, everything about him nondescript. He was expert at this, having done it many times. Drawing in a deep breath, he released all memory of past glory and immersed himself into character.

Castlebay's buildings appeared to be falling into mold and ruin. The few people he saw were thin, pale, their clothing threadbare. Even the water lapping at the shoreline looked oily, rank; the stench of rotting fish mingled with the foul putrescence of decayed potatoes. It would appear this island had not escaped the blight.

Scotland was a cursed place—he'd happily leave if he weren't so curious, and clandestinely exhilarated, about what he expected to find here.

The unpleasant tingling in his fingers and toes, the shivering that wouldn't stop, the nausea, and a plaguing headache—all the telltale physical signs were present, and they grew stronger the closer he came to this island, to the point of making him lose his breakfast over the ship's rails.

More than six hundred years had passed since he'd last seen his nemesis—Chrysaleon of Mycenae. He'd long ago played with the enticing idea that maybe Chrysaleon and his two unsuspecting hangers-on, Aridela and Menoetius, would never come back. Maybe Harpalycus was free of them at last. But as much as he wished it could be true, he knew it wasn't. He hadn't yet succeeded in ferreting out the secret that would make those three stay dead. The inalterable certainty was what kept him moving, switching bodies, staying close to the ground—that along with the hard-won knowledge of the triad's other followers. He'd never been able to sense their presence as he could the central three.

One of them could be staring at him right now.

As Prince Harpalycus, he'd believed that achieving immortality would naturally bring power and renown. He'd foreseen the entire world bowing and worshipping him. He'd thought it would be easy.

Yet here he was, wealthy but unknown, unheralded, unworshipped, thirty-four hundred years later. Lingering on the pier at Castlebay, he clenched his hands and succumbed to fury at this humiliating fact.

Long ago, Harpalycus had been forced to accept just how vulnerable he was. Being conspicuous and powerful drew attention—attention he could not afford—not as long as Chrysaleon and those who followed him walked upon the earth.

The last time he and Chrysaleon had matched wits, in the year 1233, Chrysaleon had almost succeeded in killing him. If it hadn't been for the clerical monk, lying dazed and senseless on the ground beside him, Harpalycus would be every bit as rotted right now as this island's potatoes.

Harpalycus was not immortal. He was not indestructible. He could not be reborn, like the triad. The only defense he had was to hide inside the bodies of strangers—men, preferably. Thanks to the experiments he and his slave, Proitos, had carried out, that was the easiest part. He could change bodies quickly, as long as he had some way of fatally wounding himself first. Only when he was dying could he consume another. Then, in a new body, he could stand within shooting distance of Chrysaleon and the man would never know.

Someday, his opportunity would come. He knew it—he had to believe it, or what use was all of this? One day, he would find the potion or spell that would bring permanent death to his ancient foe. He spent enormous sums of money on that goal, and hired the most evil minds he could find to resolve it. But until that day came, Harpalycus intended to enjoy himself.

As much as he despised Chrysaleon, it was worse when his old enemy was dead. Time was interminable with no opponent to thwart, no trickery to perform, no love match to destroy, no one to torture. The last six centuries had been an endless, dry desert of boredom. Now, as he gazed upon the sad little village of Castlebay, he felt excitement for the first time in eons. Chrysaleon gave him purpose. Soon, he hoped, he'd be merrily wreaking havoc and bringing misery to that other prince—the one he'd hated for so very long.

He would prolong the amusement this time. He didn't want Chrysaleon to die too quickly. He wanted to make him writhe.

Keeping his head down, the brim of his cap low, he entered the town, trying to ignore the queasy sensation of still being on water, the dip and rise of the horizon that made his stomach roil.

Where are you, prince of Mycenae? And the little one. Where is she?

Never fear. If you are hiding on this pitiful island, I will find you, hopefully before you find me.

DRINKING ESTABLISHMENTS WERE EXCELLENT SOURCES OF INFORMATION. Acquiring a dram of listless whisky, Owen sat in a dim corner and observed.

The patrons, all men, were subdued. He knew this famine had been at their throats for seven years now, off and on. Hundreds had been forced, either by hunger, poverty, or eviction, to leave.

But encouraging gossip was a simple matter of mixing whisky with a sympathetic expression. Thankfully, he could use this consumed body's Gaelic as if it were his own.

For these locals, two events were worth celebrating—the fact that in all the seven years, only two Barra residents had died of starvation, and that the island's owner, a miserly lout by the name of John Gordon, seemed to have lost his zeal for evictions.

They told him that after Gordon forcibly cleared over a thousand of his tenants in 1851, he'd then had his factor relocate eleven families from the west coast over to Balnabodach, on the east coast, where much of the clearing had taken place, and up into the rocky, barren hills, so that the fertile western areas could be rented to mainlanders at far higher rents. Had he come here to rent from Colonel Gordon?

No, Owen assured them. He was a simple homeless traveler, searching for work, trying to avoid emigration.

They grew friendlier after that, although they were quick to tell him he would find no paying labor on Barra. Several offered to put him up though, with well-known Highland hospitality.

When they asked what he was called, he knew he was close to being accepted. "Owen Anderson," he told them, proud of his authentic accent.

He'd chosen the name randomly as he boarded the ship over to Barra, dumping "Charles Kelly," the name he'd used while living in the innocuous village of Glenelg, on the mainland's west coast. Infuriating place. He'd been drawn there by the nausea, tingling, and headache, and was certain he would find Chrysaleon, but he didn't. He lingered for several months without ever encountering anyone from the distant past. It was the first time his physical reactions had failed him.

One night he took out his boredom and impatience on an easy target, a snooty bitch named Hannah something, who had unwisely chosen to wander alone at night. He cleared out the next day, before he could be linked to the crime.

Once safely away from Glenelg, he'd put himself into a deep, searching trance. An image formed in his mind, and the name. *Barra*. He'd never heard of it, and had to inquire to find out where and what it was—an island in the Outer Hebrides. That made him curse. He always tried to avoid sea travel.

The men in Castlebay's tavern shifted to bragging. Against all odds, they told him, the people displaced from their homes and forced over to the other side of the island had managed to thrive. There were fifteen families now living at Balnabodach, and two women expecting babies. Plus, they could say with some surety that this year's barley was healthy.

May God continue to show merciful forgiveness.

Owen kept his reaction to an infinitesimally lifted brow. What fools people were, easily distracted, easily manipulated. Nothing proved that better than religion. These villagers would praise God for a single season's good crop and never once blame him for the years of rot that demolished their lives.

He studied the men in the smoky room, and the two barmaids who served them, but none had any effect on him. Sometimes, when he encountered any of the triad, a momentary glow would manifest around them. Such a thing would be easy to see in this dark taproom.

None of them were here. He would have to keep searching.

"Have any of you met this Colonel Gordon?" he asked. Perhaps he was Chrysaleon.

"No, he never comes here," was the reply.

Another man said, "His factor carries out his orders." He spat on the floor, which earned him an irritated sigh from one of the barmaids.

"Who is that?" Owen asked.

"Did you see the big house on the hill outside the village?"

"It would be hard to miss."

"That's where the bastard lives, he and his whore wife and their children. Through all our suffering, they have gone about in silk and velvet, with plenty to eat and fine wine to drink."

"The blight first struck the same month she gave birth," one of the men said, shaking his finger. "Proving that God was punishing us for allowing their sin."

"Sin?" Owen asked softly.

"The slut was betrothed, morally and honorably, but her intended fell ill and died, and that very night she spread her legs for the factor. In his stables! They were caught doing it!"

"Ah," Owen said.

"They must've conspired to kill the man somehow, but there was no evidence, so nothing could be done."

Now all the patrons and the barmaids joined in, eager to denigrate the factor and his scandalous family. One barely got out a claim before another embellished it, or revealed something worse.

"The slut was born into a Catholic family, but she has never been to confession or bowed her head at Mass. She has never received the Host."

This piqued Owen's attention, but it could be a coincidence. He must find out more.

"Now they raise their weans without the blessing of baptism!"

"Her belly was getting round when they wed, if you take my meaning, but she showed no shame, went about just as she always had."

One of the men snorted. "I say they aren't wed, and never have been. He took her away, and they announced they were husband and wife when they returned. No priest on Barra would perform the ceremony."

"Aye, that ring she wears means nothing. Who among us has ever seen marriage papers?"

"The blight goes on and on, and no doubt will until someone exposes the truth—that they're living in mortal sin."

"She didn't mourn Daniel at all—"

"Daniel?"

"Her betrothed, poor orphan lad. They grew up together and he never looked at another lass. He would've died for her."

"And probably did," someone muttered.

Owen smoothed a hand over his beard to stop himself from laughing, but he quickly sobered. His own dilemma returned to the forefront of his mind as the men went on grumbling.

In order to achieve his desires, he had to find a way to kill his old adversary for good. Until he did, he was cursed to wander, to hide, to live in never-ending frustration, discontent, and thwarted dreams. He'd murdered Chrysaleon more than once, but the bastard always came back! The running started over again, the fear of being discovered, the sense of helplessness. Only when Chrysaleon was decisively, irrevocably defeated, could he rise up and do what his heritage demanded—rule this world and all who lived upon it.

I will find you, he thought, clenching his hand around the whisky glass. *I will have vengeance for all you have done to me.*

"Why did the factor go after *her?*" one of the barmaids was asking. "Any one of us would've made him a better wife. We're good Christian women, and we would've borne him weans he would know were his own."

There were nods and agreement.

Hypocritical sluts, Owen thought. *You say you hate him, yet you're vexed he didn't chase after you instead.*

"She's not even pretty, with those cold eyes. And she's rude. Why does she call her husband 'Mackinnon'? It's disrespectful, like he's a servant."

"She's half-daft, always has been. Mind you, she didn't speak a word until she was five at least."

"Don't forget she dances...to the sea!"

There was an outburst of derisive laughter.

"Thinks she's a mermaid," a man said.

"I thought her wean would come out half-fish," the other barmaid said. "A cursed pagan, that's what she is."

"No feminine modesty."

But the worst, the very worst thing, was how Aodhàn Mackinnon carried out the brutal clearings two years back. He'd hired mercenaries who beat and chained folk, threw them on board their boats to be taken away with nothing but the clothes they were wearing.

And Lilith, the whore he married, had stood on a hill *laughing!* She *laughed* at what was being done to her countrymen! She held up her daughter to watch!

"I think I'll do my best to avoid your factor and his wife," Owen said.

"You won't need to worry over that," said the man nearest him. "They've gone off," he paused dramatically, "on *holiday.*"

This provoked mutters of envy and hatred.

"Well, I am bone weary," Owen said. "I've been traveling for days. If you don't mind, I would like to rest for a fortnight or so before I leave."

"Aye, aye," the same man said, slapping his shoulder. "You're welcome to all we can give, which I'm sorry to say isn't much."

"I thank you," Owen said, bowing his head.

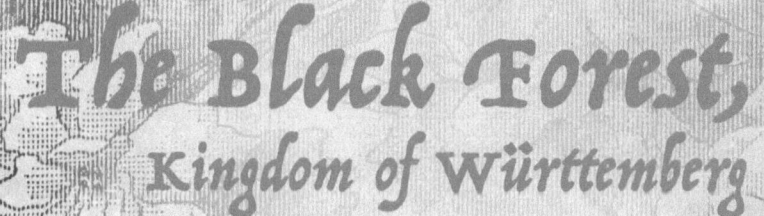

The Black Forest,
Kingdom of Württemberg

September,
1853

Chapter Twenty

Aodhàn was grateful that Lilith couldn't know how being here, in this ancient pine forest where faery tales were invented, brought back their last life together and how it had ended, early in the thirteenth century.

For her, there would be no recollection. As frustrating as it was, having to win her over and over again in every life, he was glad for that. She would never remember the sly grin on Harpalycus's face in the sanctuary at Wiesbaden, after the sentence was declared and her doom set, or being taken to the square and tied to the stake as the faggots beneath her were set aflame.

His old Cretan slave, Alexiare, always insisted that Harpalycus's existence was different than the triad's. "He doesn't die because he moves from body to body," Alexiare claimed. "If you ever recognize him, you must kill him instantly, no matter the cost. If you succeed, he will be gone, I promise you. We'll be free of him…forever."

As eager as Chrysaleon was to comply, it took thousands of years, for the devil disguised himself well and had key advantages. There was no aura to give him away, no surge of energy, like the lightning bolt. The only thing that betrayed Harpalycus was the acrid stench of ashes that clung to him, and the chaos he caused. Chrysaleon had to be very close to detect the smell, and Harpalycus was careful to prevent that from happening—until the thirteenth century, when he boldly emerged from hiding.

Living as Heinrich Baten, the Church's infamous Papal Inquisitor, he had arrested then interrogated Aridela, baiting her in front of a crowd of monks, soldiers, and priests. When he finished tormenting her, he sentenced her to the stake, all in an effort to goad Chrysaleon into revealing their love affair. The bastard would have liked nothing better than to watch them both burn, side by side—no matter that his abhorrent victory would only be temporary.

Chrysaleon kept his silence, though it was one of the hardest things he had ever done. He promised himself the right moment would come —he would save Aridela and turn Harpalycus's smirk into howls of agony. But the man was always surrounded in layers of armed guards. He even utilized a food taster. Chrysaleon couldn't get close—not until after Aridela had been tortured and put to death.

His spies informed him that Baten would be on a certain road on a certain day. Chrysaleon sent twenty loyal knights to find and slay him.

They succeeded.

"Thank you for bringing me here," Lilith said, pulling him out of haunting memories and into the present. Aodhàn heard his daughters giggling as they chased their puppy around the nearby trees.

They lay on a large blanket in a secluded clearing beside a swift-moving stream, among black firs and pines and the greenest grass he'd ever seen. Not far away was the beautiful little Schloss Aodhàn had acquired with his inheritance and some of the gratuity John Gordon had given him for handling the Balnabodach clearings.

For nearly three months, he and his family had savored their time in the Black Forest, and none had yet expressed a wish to go home.

A distant mutter of thunder floated from the west as he leaned over and kissed his wife. "You could be shopping in Paris."

She snorted.

"You're a daft, unco lass," he said, in his best Highland accent. "I think you must be a selkie, and no' a girl at all."

"Because I cannot bear crowds, stink, gossip, and noise? This is heaven, lying here, with no sound but the wind and water, and my weans laughing, and you, persecuting me."

"Persecuting you? Is that what you call it?"

"Who wouldn't? I cannot take a breath without you making your tiresome demands."

He pinioned her and tickled her until he had her gasping.

A sigh of pure, joyous relief built in his lungs. He held Lilith and placed his mouth on the side of her neck, knowing how sensitive she was at that spot. Kissing her there never failed to initiate the response he wanted.

No more Harpalycus. And, in this life at least, the threat of Menoetius eliminated.

Dare he allow himself to think it? If the last eight years were a sign, maybe he could also say *No more Athene.*

Aodhàn breathed in the clean essence of pine, tinged with rain. Reclining on his back with one arm crooked under his head, admiring the ever-changing clouds, he realized contentment had replaced the old, tightly strung tension. Astonished, he said without thinking, "I've won."

"Won what?" Lilith squinted at him.

He ran a stem of grass over her cheek. "Nothing has happened. I never let myself hope, but now I think I can."

"What are you talking about?"

"She's not going to punish me. It's been eight years."

"Eight years since what?"

"Since Daniel died, and you decided I was worthy of your love."

Her expression darkened. Her head drew back slightly. She'd never said it, but Aodhàn knew that as happy as she was with him, any thought of Daniel still brought almost unbearable pain. He caught her sometimes, holding the bronze ring Daniel had given her, staring blankly and weeping. At those times, he wasn't certain which was worse. Jealousy or guilt.

"What did you think would happen?" she asked. "Who did you think was going to punish you, and why? What did you do?"

He shrugged. "Ah, never mind. This place bewitched me for a moment. I feel I'm in a dream—or here it would be a Norse tale, I suppose."

She still frowned, until he laughed and pulled two pins out of her hair, causing it to tumble.

She curled her fingers into his cravat, drawing him closer. "Aodhàn," she whispered.

Enthralled as ever, he kissed her, but she stopped him before he could begin unbuttoning her blouse. "There's something you're not telling me," she said. "No. Don't deny it. You have nightmares, Aodhàn. All the time. You have no peace."

"And you want to fix me, like your beasties."

"Of course I do. You're in pain. D'you mind last night?"

"What about it?"

"I had to wake you. You were shouting. I thought you might frighten the children. You don't remember, do you?"

"No." He sat up, scraping back his hair, wanting to reassure her, to tell her she had fixed him, had made him whole again. But— "Where are the weans?" he heard himself say instead.

"Don't try to—wait. Where *are* they?"

He stared at Lilith and she stared back. Both scrambled up at the same time.

"Claire! Evie!"

"Claire!"

"Here, Da," came Claire's distant reply.

"That way," Lilith said. They ran towards the voice, entering the dusky shade beneath the trees. "Claire?"

"Here. Here."

"Over there, I think," Aodhàn said, taking Lilith's hand. "Come out," he called.

"No, Da," the child returned.

"What the devil?" Aodhàn pulled apart some underbrush.

Claire and Evie were squatting at the foot of a pine tree. Between them crouched another girl, a skinny, pale child, nearly naked, with a scratched and dirty face. She held Evie's puppy against her chest.

"What the devil?" Aodhàn repeated. "What is this?"

"We found her. She's alone…I think. We don't understand her."

Aodhàn knelt. "What is your name?" he asked gently. He sensed Lilith startle as this was the first time he'd spoken German around her, but she would simply think he'd learned it at Eton, and that was true, for the most part. She wouldn't remember that they'd lived north of here, six hundred years ago, or that she'd spoken the language as fluently as he, though in those days, it was altogether different.

The child gazed at him with wide, frightened eyes. "Romhilde."

"Romhilde," he repeated, smiling. "Are you lost?"

She nodded.

"Are you hungry?"

Again she nodded.

He rose. "This is Lilith," he said. "My daughters, Evie and Claire. If you will come with us, we have food."

She didn't hesitate for long, reassured by the two girls who nodded and patted her hands.

Lilith led the child to the clearing by the stream. She sat beside her on the blanket and fed her cold chicken, cheese, and rye bread from the basket they'd brought along. Claire fetched a cup of water from the stream. The begging puppy also received some chicken, which made the foundling smile.

"She's so thin," Lilith said to Aodhàn as she combed through the child's tangled hair with her fingers. "See if she'll tell you how long she's been here."

"How long have you been lost?" Aodhàn asked the girl, who was shoving food voraciously into her mouth.

She merely shrugged.

"Can you tell us who your parents are?"

She stopped chewing. The look in her eyes caused Lilith to bring the child onto her lap and hold her tight.

"What is it, *Engelchen*," Aodhàn asked her. "You're safe with us."

He listened to her broken, tearful story, asked a question now and then, and reassured her again and again that she was safe.

"I think she must have been stolen by gypsies," he told Lilith. "She says she's been with them as long as she can remember, used for labor, cooking, and cleaning. She says her guard drank too much one night, 'many nights ago,' she says, and forgot to bind her, so she ran away, and has been alone ever since."

"Poor, poor child." Lilith stroked the girl's hair. "She doesn't remember who her parents are?"

Aodhàn shook his head. "She can't even mind what they looked like. She doesn't know her last name, only "'Romhilde.'"

"Can we keep her?" Evie tugged on Lilith's arm.

"Aye," said Claire. "Can we take her home with us?" She reached out and clasped the child's dirty hand. "She needs a home."

Aodhàn regarded Lilith, who returned his gaze, brows lifted. He knew that look. Both of his daughters gazed at him, openly pleading.

The child stared at him too. Hers was the face that secured the answer.

Right or wrong, they had a third child.

The Eavesdropper

September,
1853

Chapter

Twenty-One

LILITH UNTIED HER WET APRON AND TOSSED IT ONTO A NEARBY SHRUB before gratefully dropping into a high-backed wicker chair next to Aodhàn's. She accepted the glass of wine he offered, which he'd told her was called *Liebfrauenmilch*. It was as sweet as a confection.

The warm evening, with its quiet dove calls and the heady scent of honeysuckle, soothed her mind and brought her down from the giggling, the screeching, and the soapy mess her children had made in their bath. Aodhàn ran his hand over her forearm and poured himself another glass.

"You speak German," she said.

He sent her a sideways glance. "We studied it at Eton, as well as Greek and Latin. Are they in bed?"

"Aye, bathed and tucked in, though I doubt they'll sleep." She rubbed her forehead. "Evie's already using German words, and will hardly let go of the wean's hand. She can't say Romhilde, though. She's calling her Romy."

Aodhàn smiled. "Our mother-in-making."

"Poor wee starveling. She's so thin, Aodhàn."

"You'll soon have her fattened up."

"I want to take her home with us, but shouldn't we try to find her kin?"

"How?"

"She can't be more than seven. Someone is still looking for her."

"I'll go to the village tomorrow and make inquiries."

Lilith twirled the stem of her wineglass. Did she have enough energy left to seek out more trouble? Aye, she decided. She did. "I've been wondering all day what you meant, when you said you'd won."

"Nothing. Nothing."

His whole demeanor changed. It was easy to see how her question unnerved him. "It meant something. You said it."

"I did? I don't remember."

"Mackinnon. Don't lie to me. 'She's not going to punish me,' you said. Who?"

He tipped the bottle, pouring himself a third glass of wine. Lilith set hers down, still half full. "Well?"

He shrugged, rubbed his jaw, and stared out towards the forest. In the bright rising moonlight, she saw his jaw clench.

"Does it have something to do with this?" The silver pendant glittered as she removed the chain from around her neck and dangled it between them.

His shoulders slumped and he sighed. But still he said nothing.

"I have waited a long time for you to finish the story," she said. "I want to know more about the queen who wore this. The woman as loyal as she was courageous. I want to see her palace—*Labyrinthos*—clearly in my mind. Is she the one you think can punish you?"

She waited, stiffening with shock as she watched a single tear fall down his cheek. She'd only ever seen him succumb to tears one other time, years ago, before they married.

Then he said softly, "Her name was Aridela."

EVIE PATTERED SWIFTLY DOWN THE WIDE STAIRS, SURE-FOOTED THOUGH there were no lamps lit. She ran her fingertips along the banisters, reveling in her ability to move from place to place as silent as a mouse.

Claire and Romy *wouldn't* stop talking. Evie was sleepy, but they wouldn't put out the lamp. Their voices and giggling kept her awake. Resentful of their already-close friendship, Evie ran from the room to find her mam. Mam would make them be quiet.

Her eyes filled with tears on command. She'd long known that no matter how vexed Mam was with her, tears softened her right up.

Her parents' low murmuring had floated up to Evie's open bedroom window, so she knew where they were. She ran along the corridor to the back of the Schloss and through the kitchen. She went out the postern door leading to a terrace where there was an arrangement of cushioned chairs and tables, and a glass overhang, and columns, wound with cascades of pale yellow flowers that filled the night air with a glorious smell.

Padding on her bare feet, she approached, ready with excuses and tears, if needed. But she paused as she heard what her father was saying.

"I think it was a volcano. From everything I learned at Eton, and what I was told when I traveled to Sumbawa, it matches. I met some men who saw what happened with Tambora. They described it to me, and that's how I remember it. I think the mountain on Callisti was a volcano. When it erupted, it destroyed the island, and nearly destroyed Crete as well."

Evie watched, her mouth falling open, as her father placed his hand on her mother's cheek.

"We hid underground, but not far enough. A wind, made of fire, burned us, you worse than me. Your hair was almost completely burned away. You carried the scars for the rest of your life."

Carefully, so as to make no sound, Evie dropped to the paving stones. She'd lost all desire to interrupt them. Her tears dried up.

She loved stories, and this one was good.

"WHAT IS THIS?"

It was her mother's voice bringing her up from sleep. Evie rubbed her eyes. She was lying on something hard and uncomfortable. And she was cold.

"What are you doing here?" Lilith picked her up and snuggled her close. "Why aren't you in bed?"

Memories returned slowly. "I wanted you to make Claire and Romy be quiet," Evie said. "But then I wanted to hear Da's stories."

"You were listening?"

Evie nodded. Quickly she squeezed her eyelids closed and worked on forming tears, for Mam did sound annoyed.

Ah, it worked. Fat tears rolled over her cheeks. "You were other people," she whispered. "Da said so."

Lilith hugged her and ascended the stairs. She came to the room all three children were sharing, and tucked Evie into her own bed. The other two were asleep by now.

"Were you that queen? And that lady, *Eamhair?* And that other one...I forget her name."

"You know how your da likes to tell stories," Lilith said. "That's all it was, dablet. He's our own *seanachaidh*, our tale-teller. Now go to sleep. Tomorrow you can help me make a cake."

Evie smiled. "Chocolate or lemon?"

"Which do you want?"

"Lemon."

"That sounds grand. And after, we'll play in the forest. Maybe we'll find a unicorn."

Lilith mused as she donned her nightgown. "I wonder if Daniel was a part of all this."

Aodhàn said nothing. She finished tying the ribbons on the bodice. "What is it? Why are you angry?"

"Why d'you think he had anything to do with us?"

"Because of the color and the lightning. Remember when I told you I saw colors around you, and you said the same of me? You said you saw color around Daniel, too. When I first met Daniel, I saw color around him. It was mostly blue. Remember when you showed me how you could touch me and make it feel like sparks? Daniel could do that too. I know I never told you, but it's true. Mackinnon—I wasn't trying to vex you. Why are you so angry?"

"Nobody shares what we've shared. Nobody else. Just us. You and I—we're linked, we come back, I always find you. Daniel isn't part of that, I don't care what kind of tricks he had."

"Calm yourself. I was just wondering. I know you don't like it, but he and I were close. I loved him. And in many ways, what he and I shared was similar to what you and I share. It's the truth." Her mouth slid into a sideways smile and she picked up the necklace, admiring it in the candlelight. "I think she'll cast her moon spell over us tonight," she said, and fastened it around her neck. She let down her hair, drawing it over one shoulder. "Come, *a annsachd*. Show me how Chrysaleon, the Lion of Mycenae, makes love."

Owen Bides

His

Time

October,
1853

Chapter Twenty-Two

THE STEWARD OF BARRA BROUGHT HIS FAMILY HOME IN OCTOBER, AS THE season veered toward winter and another crop of potatoes withered to slime.

Owen Anderson had his first glimpse of Aodhàn Mackinnon and his wife, Lilith, the very day they came home. He was standing on a dirt lane not far from the pier, among a group of men. Gloaming had fallen. They'd all been drinking.

"Well, will you have a look at that," said Peter Bateson, the man Owen was living with. "Barra's factor, gracing us with his presence again, at last."

Owen hardly heard the man through the headache spiking suddenly between his temples and the hum throbbing in his ears. His fingers and toes vibrated. He squinted and stepped forward, inhaling like a carnivore scenting prey.

There it was. The faintest mist-like glow, dissipating almost imme-diately.

Two of them at least, were here. That swagger suggested Chrysa-leon, and of course, the woman was Aridela. *Finally.* He'd been waiting almost four months. All this time he'd felt they were here, but they *weren't.* The same thing had happened at Glenelg, and he'd lost all patience.

He grinned.

"What is it?" Peter asked. "D'you know the man?"

"No." Owen schooled his features. "No. I was simply thinking of the tales I've heard. Now here they are, and I can see for myself."

"See the horns sprouting off his forehead, you mean?" Peter laughed.

"I thought you said they had two daughters."

"Aye, that's true."

"Then why do I see three?"

Peter whistled. "They weren't gone that long." He shook his head. "I cannot say."

"Eh, she must be a witch." Owen spoke just loud enough for Peter to hear.

The man's attention sharpened. He stared at the couple and their children, who laughed and chased a yelping puppy as though they'd known each other all their lives.

"Aye," Peter said. His tongue lingered on the word like it was made of whisky.

Owen smiled, well satisfied.

The very next day, Owen, Peter, and Peter's wife, Ivy, were enjoying a rare day of sunshine. Ivy was mending, while Owen and Peter smoked.

The youngest of the Bateson children, Moira, came running, gasping, so eager to share her news that she tripped over a half-buried stone and nearly fell.

"Evie said her mam's been other people. So has her da!"

Ivy Bateson's needle paused above her mending. "What?" She turned a puzzled gaze on her daughter.

Peter Bateson, sitting and smoking on the edge of a washtub, snorted. Owen merely relit his pipe and waited for what might come next.

"What does that mean?" Ivy's forehead creased.

Solemnly, Moira said, "She told me her mam and da don't die, or they die but then get new bodies, and different names. She said her mam was a queen once. I think that's what she said. She kept using words I didn't understand."

"She was making up one of her faery tales, then."

"No, she said it's true because she heard them talking about it and they didn't know she was there."

Ivy frowned awhile. Then she said the very thing Owen hoped she would say. "That sounds blasphemous to me. Folk live and die at God's command. After death they go to heaven, hell, or purgatory. You know this, Moira Bateson. Any mortal, man or woman, who could break that rule would be of the Devil's making—a witch or some other evil. I don't want you seeing that child anymore. D'you hear? She's lying. She's trying to fool you and make you believe in unnatural things."

"Aye, Mam," Moira said, frightened and chastised.

Ivy went back to her mending with a darkly spoken, "Those weans are changelings, through and through. I've always said so."

Owen turned his gaze to Peter, who was staring back at him, his face rigid with horrified suspicion. Lifting his hands, Owen slowly shook his head to indicate his own shock.

How easy it was to direct the fates of others, even when they were watched over by a goddess.

NOVEMBER PROVIDED A GOOD DAY HERE AND THERE, WITH WATERY sunshine and sharp breezes that stimulated the mind. Lilith loved the bite of winter as much as the mildness of summer, and never wasted fine weather. Believing that fresh sea air was good for the health and appetite of all children, she took them to play along the bluffs overlooking the sea. Faith often went along, though she wasn't one to play or dance. Instead, she preferred to find a flat rock and gaze at the water. Lilith often wondered if she was thinking of Stuart, but she never asked, not wanting to dredge up sad memories.

The first time they took Romy to the coast, the child was mesmerized by it, as she had been on the Channel crossing, and the boat ride from the mainland to Barra. Like Faith, she loved sitting and watching its ceaseless movement and changing color.

"She looks like a faery," Faith said. "I expect to see wings sprout from her shoulders."

"Aye," Lilith agreed. "Or a nymph. She's our mountain child, an *oread*. Aodhàn's been teaching me the myths from Greece."

"She seems happy."

"I think she is, now that we're starting to understand each other."

"They learn fast at that age."

"Claire and Romy prattle away without any trouble."

"But Evie."

"Aye," Lilith said, laughing. "Now there's a mishmash."

Romhilde knew a good amount of Gaelic by now, and some English. Claire had no trouble learning German. But when Evie grew excited, her speech emerged in a jumble of three different languages, which confused Faith, Greyson, and even Lilith at times.

Bringing home an orphan from Europe only worsened the factor's reputation. Why hadn't he taken in some hungry Barra child if he wanted to adopt? Why was a foreigner singled out for rescue? It proved he had nothing but contempt for the people he'd lived among for so long.

"I think of her kin," Faith said. "Did Aodhàn really try to find them?"

"Aye, he went throughout the region, asking. But gypsies travel long distances. She could've come from anywhere, really. I suppose, after a week, I didn't really want him to find anyone. We love her."

"You've always taken in lost, injured creatures. She's no different."

"She is different. She's a girl."

Faith shrugged. "You're happy as well, aren't you?"

"I am." Lilith was surprised. It was uncharacteristic for Faith to show concern for something as ephemeral as happiness. The way she stumbled over the question betrayed how uncomfortable she was asking it.

"What of you, Mam? Are you happy?"

Her mother pulled up a fistful of wind-bent grass and shrugged. "I've never had a notion what happiness is. I want you to know something. I saw how Aodhàn looked at you, even when you were children. I conspired with him, almost from the first. Mind when I sent you back to Bishop House for my mending?"

"Oh, Mam. I know all this."

Faith scowled as she met Lilith's amused gaze. "It's true I hoped you would end up his wife. But I had nothing to do with what happened to Daniel. You don't think that, do you?"

"I never thought that. It was the miasma."

Faith turned back to the sea and for some time, she said nothing. Her face was like stone, sharply etched and blank. Then, after biting her lip, she said, "I suppose I should tell you that going off like you did, and coming home with another child, made them hate you even more."

"They decided to hate me the moment I wed Aodhàn. Sometimes I think they decided to hate me the instant I was born. No one ever cared about Daniel until he died, and I fell in love with the factor's son. Then, of course, they were all Daniel's comrades, and I was the whore who betrayed him. There's nothing I could ever do to change it. I don't care and never have."

Claire called to her then. Lilith smiled reassuringly at Faith and went off to see what her daughter had found.

Falling From Grace

November, 1853

Chapter

Twenty-Three

Lɪʟɪᴛʜ ʟᴏᴠᴇᴅ sᴘᴇɴᴅɪɴɢ ʜᴇʀ ᴅᴀʏs ɴᴇᴀʀ ᴛʜᴇ ᴡᴀᴛᴇʀ, ʙᴜᴛ sɪɴᴄᴇ Aᴏᴅʜàɴ had shared the fantastic tale of their past lives, she couldn't get enough of him. It was incredible, enticing, the idea that they'd returned from death, and that he had only ever wanted and loved her, of all the women he must have known through the centuries.

They found every out-of-the-way nook at Bishop House, and once even made love in the secret passageway. Later, when Evie complained of hearing ghosts moaning in the walls, Lilith was both amused and mortified, and refused to repeat that adventure for fear of causing her children emotional harm.

She asked for more stories from their other lives, hoping at some point she would remember them herself. Sometimes flashes came to her, as they always had, but now they made sense, these piecemeal remnants. They were moments from a real, lost past, strong enough to remain in her mind, but not quite strong enough to clarify into definable memories.

But Aodhàn didn't like talking about the past. His reluctance was obvious. She didn't understand it, when everything he'd told her was beautiful and pleasant, but for the one calamity of the volcanic eruption, which left her scarred, and, apparently, nearly without hair. Yet, as he told it, she recovered, went on to live many more years, and led her people back to comfort and plenty.

"Why are we born, again and again?" she asked. "Does it happen to everyone? Why do you remember, and I don't?"

He became noticeably uncomfortable at those questions, and would only say he didn't know. Sometimes she wondered if he was deliberately withholding details from her.

Every now and then, she would ask, narrow-eyed, "Are you making this all up? Because I will slice off your balls, Aodhàn Mackinnon, if you are," which always made him laugh.

"What did I look like? What did you look like? How did we meet?"

He didn't mind questions like that as much. His eyes acquired a haze of nostalgia as he described her, and her country, and the costumes the women wore, and her mother's amazing arboretum, where she kept lions. He told her about the delegations from Egypt, laden with gifts of linen, ivory, papyrus, and their rare beautiful wood that was good not only for sculpting and furniture, but also for treating fevers and women's birthing pain.

She wore the necklace every day. It helped her envision the amazing island of Crete, its legendary queen, and the queen's beloved consort. She had a superstitious hunch that the necklace possessed a kind of protective magic that would keep everyone she loved safe.

The opposite seemed to be true for Aodhàn, though. Since he'd told her his long-held secrets, he was clearly on edge and not sleeping well. She tried to impart reassurance in her caresses.

I love you. I will always be here.

OWEN BOUGHT HIS COMRADES ANOTHER ROUND OF WHISKY. HE'D BECOME quite popular over the last few months, as he always seemed to have enough coin to provide his friends a dram or two. He was being especially generous tonight.

"There will never be a good crop of potatoes until we cleanse Barra of pestilence," Peter Bateson said. He'd already shared his daughter's gossip about Evie and her kin. "'Tis a clear message, if you ask me. The potatoes rot, year after year, just as Barra rots from the evil we allow."

"Remember Daniel," one of the other men said.

There was much nodding, muttering, and the sign of the cross being made.

Owen gestured to the barmaid to bring more whisky.

"It's clear now why she never goes near a priest," the barmaid said as she poured. "No doubt she'd burst into flames."

"A witch," whispered the other barmaid. "Here on Barra!"

"I heard Gordon rewarded him for the beatings and clearings at Balnabodach," Peter said. "The factor's a wealthy man now. Rich, in fact."

"Mind you how she laughed at those poor souls that day?" Whoever spoke was slurring.

The time has come, Owen thought, and stood. All eyes turned to him.

"Who's with me, men?" he asked. "It's time to bring Barra back into Heaven's good graces. Are you tired of being hungry, of your wives and weans being sick and unhappy?"

"Aye," the men said, lifting their glasses.

"But what can we do?" Peter asked.

"What has to be done. This must be the reason God drew me here. I can lead you! God requires brave warriors, not milksops. It's long past time Barra was cleansed of evil...of witchcraft."

There was that word. It flew from his lips and hissed over the room, skewering through each man like the blade of a flaming sword. They looked at each other then rose, roaring with drunken fervor.

LILITH HAD SUSPECTED SOMETHING FOR A WHILE. NOW THAT SHE WAS sure, she managed to scrape together the ingredients for Aodhàn's favorite sponge cake. Sending the girls away to play, she brought out a bottle of German wine, which caused him to raise a brow.

"I'm going to have a baby," she said, holding back her elation until his own reaction was clear.

It was immediate. He leaped up and grabbed her, pulling her to her feet. Wrapping her in his arms, he held her head to his chest and laughed. The sound, though muffled, was exultant. Delighted.

"You're pleased?" She struggled to free her head so she could look into his face. When she did, she was a little surprised, for his eyes were fiercely incandescent. "Surely you're tired of children by now," she said, teasing.

He covered her face with kisses before whispering, "I have never been so happy. Never. And that's saying something."

For a moment she saw his colors again, vibrant red, and the luxuriant orange of a sunset over the ocean. She felt the singular sparking sensation flow from his fingertips into her skin.

He pulled his head back from hers, saying, "There's your colors. Gold and pale purple."

"I see yours too. Does it mean something? Will this child be special?"

"Of course." He grinned as he recovered his usual composure. "Have you forgotten the Mackinnon motto? 'Fortune favors the bold.' Tell me—dare I hope for a son?"

"You may dare," she replied, "but don't get set on it."

"You intend to smother me in girls," he complained.

They took the bottle of wine into the drawing room. Aodhàn wanted to make love before the fire, but Lilith insisted he wait until the children were in bed.

"This is just the beginning," she said. "Think of it, our weans, growing up, marrying, and having wee weans of their own."

"We'll be grandparents," he said, as though the idea had never occurred to him before. He sounded quite amazed, which made her laugh.

"I want to leave this place," she said. "Tell John Gordon of Cluny to hire another factor. I don't want my children growing up here, Aodhàn, amongst all this hate. I've no more patience for the way they've been slighted and abused."

Loud banging on the front door echoed through the house.

"Who could that be, so late?" Lilith asked, sitting up.

The children came running down the stairs to see who was there. Claire peered out the front window as Cora, the maid, went to open the door.

"Mam, there's a great lot of men outside," Claire said.

"What now?" Lilith sighed. "I was just going to put the girls to bed."

"I'll write Gordon tomorrow," Aodhàn said. He drew up a handful of his wife's dark hair, and rubbed his cheek on it. "You and I," he said, low. "For as long as the pyramids stand in Egypt."

THE END

Historical Notes

Quote from *Wuthering Heights*, by Emily Brontë: When *Wuthering Heights* was first published in 1847, the author was listed as Ellis Bell: that's why Lilith refers to the author as "he."

Short quote from *A Christmas Carol*, by Charles Dickens.

The Mackinnon family, and the "factor of Barra," is fictitious, my invention, and bears no resemblance to anyone, living or dead.

I also took a few liberties with the coastline and caves on Mingulay, although the cliffs there are quite impressive, and a popular rappelling destination.

"Bishop House," on Barra, is my invention, as is the house on Mingulay.

Allt Easdail is the local name of an archaeological site on southern Barra, an area that appears to have been used and built upon since Neolithic times.

The less said the better about John Gordon of Cluny.

Titles in The Child of the Erinyes Series

To the Reader

Thanks for reading *The Moon Casts a Spell!* I hope you enjoyed it.

Connect with me and read lots of extras at my website, where I have:
    Bibliographies
    Maps
    Purchase links
    Histories
    Character details

rebeccalochlann.com

About the Author

While growing up, Rebecca Lochlann began envisioning an epic story, a new kind of myth, one built upon the foundation of the Greek classics and continuing through the centuries right up into the present and future.

This has become her life's work, though she didn't exactly intend it to be that way when she started.

The Child of the Erinyes series is mythic fantasy, inspired by the Greek tale of Ariadne, Theseus, and the Minotaur. As one reader put it, "Loads of testosterone, slaughter, and crazy magic," with a love story, of course.

Though the story is fiction-fantasy, it still took about fifteen years to research the Bronze Age segments of the series, and encompassed rare historical documents, mythology, archaeology, ancient religions, and volcanology.

The Year-god's Daughter is her debut novel: Book One of *The Child of the Erinyes* series. It has been utilized as a study guide in an American university, named a B.R.A.G. Medallion honoree, and was a finalist in the Chaucer Historical Fiction awards. Book Two, *The Thinara King*, a First Place winner in the Ancient History category of the Chaucer Historical Fiction awards and a Next Generation Indie Book Awards finalist, continues the saga. Book Three, *In the Moon of Asterion*, wraps up the Bronze Age segment of the series and leads into the middle trilogy, set in Scotland. These are: Book Four, *The Moon Casts a Spell*, Book Five, *The Sixth Labyrinth*, and Book Six, *Falcon Blue*, which jumps backward in time to the Early Medieval Era.

The denouement comes in the final three books: *When the Moon Whispers, First and Second Chronicles*, and *Swimming in the Rainbow*.

Rebecca has always believed that certain rare individuals, either blessed or tortured, voluntarily or involuntarily, are woven by fate or the Immortals into the labyrinth of time, and that deities sometimes speak to us through dreams and visions, gently prompting us to tell their lost stories. Who knows? It could make a difference.

Connect with Rebecca at her website, BookBub, Facebook, or in a review at your point of purchase.

Attributions

My author website has maps, bibliographies, and more: rebeccalochlann.com

Front and back cover designs: Rebecca Lochlann, Erinyes Press
    Original front cover images, *The Moon Casts a Spell* and *The Sixth Labyrinth*: Eve Ventrue, eve-ventrue.com

Back Cover *The Moon Casts a Spell* Print Edition:
    Starry Night Sky: jonson, Depositphotos
    Labyrinth: EcOasis, Shutterstock

Original title page image: Anna Ismagilova, Shutterstock

Labrys Axe graphic © "Labrys-symbol" Licensed under Public domain via Wikimedia Commons http://commons.wikimedia.org/wiki/File:Labrys-symbol.svg#mediaviewer/File:Labrys-symbol.svg

Crescent moon, necklace image & Erinyes Press logo: Lance Ganey freelanceganey.com/

The Sixth Labyrinth
EXCERPT

If you enjoyed *The Moon Casts a Spell* and would like to see what happens next, please look for the fifth installment.

The Sixth Labyrinth

Morrigan Lawton lives a lonely, wearying existence in a land that long ago turned its back on magic and myth.

Curran Ramsay enjoys every advantage and is loved by all who know him. Yet none of his successes can rid him of the sense that he is missing something, or someone. It haunts every moment, awake and in dreams.

Twenty years ago, the sea stole Aodhàn Mackinnon's memories and nearly drowned him. Now a penniless fisherman, his heart reels from an agony he cannot quite remember--until the landowner's new wife comes to Glenelg.

A silenced but enduring goddess has seen her place in the souls of mortals systematically destroyed.

But she bides her time.

For Athene, thousands of years mean nothing.
Ancient prophecy and the hand of a goddess propel the triad into the winding corridors of *The Sixth Labyrinth*.

The sea claims final possession, and leaves nothing behind.

The Sixth Labyrinth, Prologue

"It looks to be a hard labor," Beatrice said.

Isabel squinted at the woman from the corner of her eye. Beatrice Stewart never wasted words. If she opened her mouth to say *It looks to be a hard labor*, well, it was no doubt going to be the worst labor ever seen in Inverness-shire.

The forest pressed in, heavy and watchful, the shadowed trees looming like baleful black giants.

Beatrice seized Isabel's arm. "Fetch water."

Grateful for a distraction from brooding thoughts and growing panic, Isabel carried a wooden bucket to the nearby burn, using a fallen tree limb to break the ice. She wasn't so far away that she couldn't hear Hannah Lawton's awful moaning as the poor lass struggled to give birth. The babe was a full two months early. Nothing could save it. They'd be lucky to save the mother, with no midwife.

She fought off tears as she knelt to fill the bucket. Hannah had endured much this day. So had the rest of Glenelg. The entire village, Isabel's friends and kin, all those she'd ever known, had been evicted, forced to watch without recourse as every building, even the old kirk, was burnt to the ground. The men hired to carry out the landlord's wishes had inflicted many cruelties. Terror, devastation, and now this unrelenting cold—brought by the worst storm she could remember blanketing the entire coast in snow—surely these things would curse the coming infant and its mother.

The bucket was cracked, but didn't seem to leak. Isabel tripped through frozen loam, snow, and hidden tree roots, handing it to Beatrice then standing there, not knowing what else to do. She glanced through bare branches and sweeping evergreen limbs into an ominous patchwork of clouds. *Lord, help this woman*, she prayed. *Help us all.*

If God ignored her, they would die, either of slow starvation or painful freezing. How many days could this pitiful band survive? Her instincts declared, *Not many.*

Hannah screamed, "Seaghan! Seaghan!" The circling trees magnified her cry.

Isabel looked at each of her companions, those who had gathered here after the destruction of their homes. Yesterday, over two hundred people lived in and around Glenelg. Now she counted seventeen. Six were children.

She turned away, not wanting these wounded, weary souls to see the defeat she couldn't hide, or her conviction that they would all die here together.

WAKE UP, DAUGHTER.

Isabel rose on one elbow, rubbing at her eyes. Mist eddied, eerie and opaque. She half-expected a unicorn or dwarf to appear.

A miracle comes. Why do you sleep?

Shivers ran over her, though she was oddly warm. "Miracle?" She peered in every direction, though she was almost certain the source of the voice was inside her own head.

The mist split like a tattered sail, framing a woman who observed her in a curious yet arrogant way. A lady with long, curling black hair and pale skin, rather like an Irish lass. But she wasn't dressed like any Irishwoman Isabel had ever seen. A narrow silver band ran across her forehead; in the center was an ornament shaped like a boat with high-pointed prow and stern, or a crescent moon propped on its spine. Her white gown, sleeveless and bound with silver ribbons, rippled about her ankles. Isabel, who loved fabric and needlework, couldn't help admiring such an uncommon article of clothing, or a twinge of envy at how it fit.

The holy child comes.

Envy vanished beneath apprehension. "Who are you?"

Handmaid of Areia Athene, she who brings life and death to men. The crown flashed as the lady inclined her head. *She brings life now, sacred life. Wake. See the child who suffers for your sake.*

"Suffers? For me?"

For you and all miserable mankind. Though you cursed and abandoned her, my Mistress loves you still. She returns her daughter, who will live among you as she prepares for her future destiny. Here, in the sixth life, she shall be known as Morrigan, the very name my Lady was called in these islands once, though few now living remember it, any more than they remember her, for she has long been discarded in favor of newer gods.

Isabel wanted to listen to this woman for the rest of her life. Pure, warm as spring breezes, her melodious voice cast away fear as well as hopelessness. But the phantasm was undulating as though she stood behind a waterfall.

"Wait!" Isabel cried.

You were once a queen, and gave her life. Grace and forgetfulness surrounds you for that. Go and look upon her. She is the finest miracle you will ever see.

Isabel sat up with a startled gasp. Someone had thrown a frayed cloth over her. It sagged around her waist as she stared wildly. Where was she? Why was it so cold? There was no mist. No lady. She'd simply had a dream.

Light from the nearby fire sent shadows dancing across the face of her brother's ill-fated wife. The woman's moans recalled tales of the *bean-sìth*, ghostly female spectres who appeared, shrieking, when someone was about to die.

Beatrice knelt between Hannah's legs. Isabel's mother was there too, her hand cupped over Hannah's knee.

It all returned in a torrent. The storm. The stench of flaming thatch. Screaming children. Folk ejected violently from their homes. One of the landlord's hired outlaws had shoved Hannah, causing her to fall. She'd landed hard on her belly.

Isabel's brother, Douglas, refused to let them board the ship for Nova Scotia. He'd said he would not be cast off like rotted fish, nor so easily forgotten. Instead he'd dragged them to this forest, and who could say in the end which choice would turn out worse?

His wife's labor had gone on and on now, for hours. Isabel had smoothed Hannah's hair and murmured nonsense meant to convey encouragement. At some point, there came a time of silence, of stillness. Hannah fell into sleep or unconsciousness and eventually, Isabel drifted off as well.

Now the labor was intensifying again. Something was wrong. The two women helping Hannah wore worry on their faces like black storm clouds on the summit of Ben Nevis.

"Why did you do this to me?" Hannah muttered. "I hate you."

Isabel said, "Wheesht, dear, you'll be fine," and stroked her cheek, but Douglas had heard.

"*A shiùrsach!*" The father of the coming child leaned over his wife, his hands bunched into fists as though he meant to strike her. "You and Seaghan thought you could make a fool of me. Now see where you are. You've made your bed—"

"Stop!" It was wee Nicky, Douglas's son by his first wife. He was only three, but he broke away from the man who held him and ran forward bravely. "Don't hurt her!" He began to sob.

Isabel had always been afraid of Douglas. She was afraid now, but she swore if that fist rose, she would put herself between them. If Nicky could stand up to him, then so, by God, could she. Bad enough to call your wife a whore to her face while she was giving birth to your child.

But Douglas turned away. He picked up his son and carried him off into the dark.

Hannah sounded like a beast caught in a steel trap, the kind that broke bones and left its captive to die in agony. Her hair hung lank. Strands clung to her thin, pale face, and her eyes were huge, black with terror. Was this what giving birth did to a woman? By the good Lord in Heaven, Isabel would never make such a mistake. No man could speak sweetly enough to make it worthwhile.

Douglas returned without Nicky and reached out, catching Beatrice's arm. Isabel started to rise, intending to throw herself over Hannah. But, "Save her," was all he said, his voice hoarse. "Don't let her die."

Isabel stared. Never in her life had she heard such misery in Douglas Lawton's voice. She couldn't trust her own ears. Perhaps he did care, after all.

"I'll do my best." Beatrice brushed his cheek with her fingertips, turning back to Hannah without expression when Douglas jerked away from her touch.

Gloaming crept into frigid night. "Saint Brigit spare the lass," one of the villagers cried, making the sign of the cross.

Beatrice slapped Hannah. "Push, or this wean'll kill you!"

Hannah sucked in a deep breath and bore down, screaming.

Desperation glimmered in the women's eyes. They moved swiftly now, sweat dappling their foreheads, though above them, ice encased the tree limbs. Blood slicked their arms to the elbows.

Hannah's flush faded to greenish-white.

At last the babe was born. The cord was cut and Isabel's mother smacked it on the rump, prompting a shaky yowl. Beatrice fought to stem Hannah's bleeding while Isabel's mother swaddled the newborn in a scrap of singed blanket.

"Ibby," her mother said, "hold this child."

Hannah's eyelids fluttered. She opened her mouth and tried to speak, but no sound came.

Black clots of blood splattered the snow. There was a hot earthy smell. Steam rose from between the new mother's legs. Isabel's empty belly lurched when Beatrice wiped sweat from her forehead, leaving behind a glistening streak of scarlet.

Back in the spring, before all these troubles, Isabel had watched Hannah wade in a mountain burn, her skirts kilted above her knees, hair trailing in the water. Laughing, she'd flicked the wet ends at some enraptured lad. With her rich red hair, wicked blue eyes, and voluptuous body, she'd left great men fair stammygastered.

It remained a mystery why this bonny girl had accepted Seaghan MacAnaugh's proposal only to break the engagement and marry Douglas Lawton instead, without waiting even the barest interval to save Seaghan's wounded pride.

Gossip had enflamed the village. Snatches trailed through Isabel's brain as she held the baby and regarded her sister-in-law.

She's a slut.

Seaghan is well rid of her, and Black Douglas Lawton has finally got what he deserves. Hope he takes her far from Glenelg.

Nothing remained now of Glenelg but smoldering ruins. Burned, like their grasping landlord wanted, cleared of crofts and bothersome humans, ready for an influx of more profitable sheep. Almost everyone Isabel had ever known, including Seaghan MacAnaugh, had sailed away to a country on the other side of the ocean. She'd never see any of those folk again. Her village, her world, had been pared down to fewer than twenty people.

Douglas kissed Hannah's forehead. *"Beannachd leat, a ghràidh,"* he said, and drew the blanket over her face.

Isabel cradled the newborn. Wee thing, light as down. Her niece. Fluids, blood, and pasty goo covered the baby's skin. Her elfish crimson face screwed into a plaintive whine.

"My sister would no' want us sniveling over her," Beatrice snapped. "Give me the child, Isabel."

Unnerved by the woman's scowl, Isabel handed the babe over.

Beatrice unwrapped the blanket. "She appears healthy, though born before her proper time. Come, Douglas, see your daughter."

Douglas, still kneeling beside his wife, glanced up. After a moment, he took the baby. He looked confused, like he'd already forgotten the cause of Hannah's death.

"Would you name her Morrigan, after our mother?" Beatrice asked.

The wee one's cry was weak and pitiful, bringing tears to Isabel's eyes. Douglas returned her to Beatrice, shrugging. "It doesn't matter."

Morrigan.

Isabel crossed herself.

The Reunion

The Sixth Labyrinth
CHAPTER ONE

Stranraer, Scotland

1872

Morrigan crouched behind a boulder, willing herself to vanish into it. She heard a scrape, as of a shoe against stone, and tensed. Silence descended, so deep and thick it beat against her eardrums.

With a sharp flutter and startled cry, a grouse rose from the sedges to her left. She squinted, trying to make out details, but all was disguised in predawn shadows.

There was no time for hesitation. She must be bold. Drawing in a breath, she leaped, loosing a warlike shout, and slapped the flat of her blade against the tall dark figure standing with his back to her. He toppled, breaking apart in a most unwarrior-like fashion. She stared. Her Viking attacker was nothing but a crude stook of weeds, roped together like a massive corn dolly and propped upright.

A hand squeezed her shoulder, bringing her around with a stifled shriek. "Thought you had me, didn't you?"

"Damn," she said.

"Don't you know by now you'll never best me? You're a female, cursed by God and nature. Sneaky, that's what you are, just like your hair, until the sun comes out and reveals the truth. Lucky for you Scotland has many cloudy days."

She couldn't help it—she nudged her braid over her shoulder and out of sight almost guiltily.

Nicholas Lawton's sardonic laughter echoed into the heavens. "No one with any wit is fooled," he said. "Red hair on a lass is unlucky, and dark red's the worst."

Nicky never tired of these well-worn taunts. Having learned long ago that to argue only worsened things, Morrigan changed the subject. "Where were you?" She dropped her clumsy wooden sword on the ground, disgusted with it, herself, and most of all, her smug brother.

"Here...there...in the sky, the ground...." He poked her chest. "In your soul." He hooked his thumbs under his braces, cocky as a Spanish matador, then plunged his own sword into the damp soil, where it quivered like a naked girl.

Nicky polished his nails on the front of his grimy sark and threw out another round of derisive laughter. It echoed off cotton-wisp clouds and frightened a covey of partridges from their nests.

Goaded to fury, Morrigan bent and grabbed her sword. She thwacked at her brother, longing to rattle his unquenchable amusement, or at least inspire his respect, but he caught her around the waist, lifted her with no apparent effort, and, dodging the blade, tossed her into a patch of gorse.

She shrieked again.

He dusted his hands, planted them on his hips, and grinned. His teeth flashed briefly, framed as they were by ill-shaven cheeks covered in black stubble. "Mind what I tell you," he said, shaking a finger before whistling at his horse. "The world's designed for men, so you're pretty much buggered." He swung onto his nag and perused the sky.

A sharp throb diverted Morrigan's attention as she untangled herself from the gorse. She knew what it was even before she looked. A thorn, embedded in her right index finger.

She pried it out, watching a crimson drop of blood balloon from the puncture.

When the gorse is not in flower, love is out of season. So the saying went.

Instead of calling him some name he would only laugh at, she heard herself say, "Is that the way of love then, bonny, sweet, yet ready to sting when you least expect?"

He looked puzzled until he saw the blood. "If you don't get home to your chores, you'll never have the chance to find out." His ready grin held a hint of devilry, as though he half-hoped she would defy their da and his temper.

"I'll be back before the train comes. Stay, Nicky. I'll read you the tale of the labyrinth, and the black Minotaur. There's plenty of time."

"Jesus, one of these days you'll fancy yourself Helen of Troy and we'll have to put you in an asylum." He leaned towards her. "Truth is, your head is full of mince. You're far more trouble than use." He shrugged. "Don't greet to me about your bruised backside. You make your own bad fortune like you cannot bear a day of peace."

That was Nicky, always trying to protect her from their father's wrath. But in the end, he never told her what to do. He let her make her own choices.

As he galloped away, Morrigan opened her satchel and pulled out her beloved, dog-eared book, *A Translated Greek Mythology*. She settled on the grassy slope overlooking Loch Ryan, glancing with appreciation at the water's indigo surface. "In truth, I'd love a day of peace," she said, studying the sky, where a rosy blush trellised the eastern horizon, sweet with promise. It couldn't yet be seven. The first train, on the Port Road from Castle Douglas, didn't arrive till eight-thirty. Papa was in his fields, where he went every morning before dawn. As long as she made it home before him, he would never know she'd left at all.

Widdie pricked her ears and nickered after Morrigan's brother. The sound was half-wistful, and the way the mare swung her head around and stared at Morrigan suggested reproof. Oh, she was imagining too much again. A reproving horse? Nicky loved to claim pagan faery blood ran through his sister's veins, and this was what caused folk to stare at her in confusion half the time, lifting their eyebrows and giving each other those *I told you, didn't I* glances.

Sometimes it did feel like she'd come from the stars rather than the Highlands. Perhaps she suffered from insanity as Nicky often suggested...but she preferred to think herself possessed by magic spells.

Maybe Hannah Stewart Lawton had been in truth a faery, a changeling...a witch. That would explain Papa's reasoning in never allowing anyone to speak of her, or of their old life in the North Country. Could she be living up there still, enchanting virile men in the forest, making them forget their pious Christian roots? Maybe, just maybe, the sorceress had managed to bequeath a few fey tricks to her daughter. Tricks the wild girl who lived inside Morrigan used often enough. That hidden, depraved lass caused nothing but trouble for hapless Morrigan, daring her to while away hours on the cliffs and moor and goading her into flirting with the lads in town. The girl's fierce voice proclaimed these rules and constraints no more than muck to be shoveled away. The two Morrigans battled incessantly, the secret one haranguing her to mischief, while the other, the outer Morrigan, longed to make everyone, especially Douglas, happy and proud.

Impossible task. No one could please him.

Morrigan opened the book and ran her fingers over the faded lettering. Papa's sister, Isabel, had given it to her on her tenth birthday. The title page held a message, written in fine, trembly script.

Someone once called you the finest miracle I'll ever see, and I've come to believe it. I was told yours is the name of a goddess, dear Morrigan. So here is a book about Greek gods and goddesses. Perhaps you will see yourself in these ancient tales.

Page sixty-seven, to which the book opened naturally, carried the chapter heading "Theseus and the Minotaur of Crete." Though she'd read it hundreds of times, the names *Theseus, Minotaur,* and *Crete* still awakened a faint involuntary shiver.

Theseus was young, the account began, *when shipped along with six other youths and seven maidens to the isle of Crete as slave-payment to King Minos. These doomed prisoners were to be fed to the gruesome Minotaur — half-man, half-bull, the product of an ungodly physical union between Minos's wife, Pasiphaë, and a magnificent white bull sent by the god Poseidon.*

Morrigan pictured the scene: lasses weeping as dark-skinned Cretan soldiers prodded them onto the vessel. Heroic Theseus, though, would never give in to such weakness.

Chewing on a fibrous stem of grass, she rested her head in the crook of one arm, hearing the enticing murmur of weeds. *Stay…relax… dream.* She closed her eyes and slipped into the old familiar fantasy of beloved Greek characters and their grand adventures.

The Athenian prince swaggered off the Cretan pier, not bothering to hide his contempt. Among those watching was Minos's daughter, Princess Ariadne, who would soon fall in love with this barbarian from the northern lands. Could she help it, when moonlight and magic brought a god's statue to life, transforming it into the foreigner's likeness? As it crossed the clearing it changed from cold marble to living man, and this man lay upon her like a lover. *For longer than you can imagine*, he promised, *I will be with you, in you, of you. Together we bring forth a new world, and nothing will ever part us. Aridela, open your heart.*

Morrigan settled more comfortably into her grassy nest. The statue called the princess Aridela, not Ariadne. Yet Morrigan knew it was no mistake. Aridela was the older name, the origin from which transpired the fable of Ariadne. She also knew, though she couldn't remember how, that Aridela's father was listed in the oracle logs as Damasen, royal consort who met his death bravely, that her mother was Helice, renowned queen of Crete, and her sister the courageous Iphiboë.

Morrigan loved to pretend she was Aridela, her hair no longer giving hints of unlucky auburn highlights but black as night-sky, her eyes not brown but exotic ebony, lined with a substance that made them appear mysterious and seductive. As Aridela, she watched the marble statue transmute into a living being. How wonderful he felt, stone warming into smooth flesh against hers, breath ardent and sweet on her cheek. She would love him forever. For as long as wayfaring stars sailed the midnight sky.

For as long as the pyramids stand in Egypt.

Morrigan scrambled from her springy bed, blinking to clear her sight. The hillside was empty but for her pony and a foraging pair of linnets, which flew up, crying in alarm at the human's sudden movement.

She must have fallen asleep and dreamed the words…but they'd sounded clear and close, as if a man spoke right next to her. Maybe the loch washing against the shore had done it. The sea could make uncanny sounds.

Reassured, she lay back in the grass and closed her eyes. It was a bonny saying. Aye, the princess would love her Theseus that long, maybe longer.

She sighed. Now she was in an arena. Hot sand burned the soles of her feet. Rising onto her toes, she ran, buoyed with the lightness of a butterfly, the swift danger of a wasp. The gate creaked behind her. A snort, heavy and challenging, was followed by the thud of massive hooves. *Aridela!* the people thundered.

She turned, laughing. The bull trotted into view. *Her* bull. It pawed the sand and lowered its head.

The crowd's chants lengthened into a continuous roar as she ran towards her destiny, what her people called *moera*.

The bull's breath heated her face then vanished as she soared, propelled by the upward jerk of his head. She turned a graceful somersault, losing herself in the rush of wind. Everything slowed. Cheers echoed, fading into an angry snort that reverberated through her eardrums. There was an instant of vertigo as the sky yawed below and sand stretched above. Then she righted herself, landing on the bull's hindquarters, her toes searching for hold in its bristly hair. She made a quick, final leap into the arms of her primped and painted half brother, who placed her safely on the ground and made a grand flourish to impress the audience. What was his name? *Isandros.*

The cheering and foot-stomping intensified until she thought the bullring would collapse. Only her mother, the queen, refused to join in.

Aridela…Aridela…Daugh…terrrrr of the Calesssiennnda!

Morrigan started, blinking against bright light striking her full in the face. There it came again. Shrill, accusatory, the whistle shivered over the moor, announcing the train as it raced to Stranraer. She should be at the Wren's Egg, helping Aunt Beatrice prepare breakfast. If hungry travelers came to the inn and she wasn't there, her da would be furious.

But what did it matter? He was always furious, no matter what she did.

Widdie nuzzled her cheek with damp, grass-stained nostrils. "We're late." Morrigan rose, brushing at the weeds and thistle clinging to her wool skirt. The sky had gone as pale as a shallow bowl of water. Looking at it, she knew with a sinking sense of dread that she would be flayed livid.

She mounted her pony and headed for the inn on Neptune Street. Then she paused. She was already damned. Why not make a pleasant memory for later, after the thrashing?

Kicking the mare to a gallop, she careened along the ridge above the loch, pretending she and Theseus were escaping enemy soldiers, making for a ship that would carry them to a secret bothy on the hazy isle of Ailsa Craig, where none would ever find them.

"Hurry or they'll catch us," she cried, looking over her shoulder at imaginary pursuers.

A gust of wind tugged at her green velvet hat, the one Aunt Isabel had given her last November for her eighteenth birthday. It flew into the air, long plaid ribbons fluttering.

Morrigan pulled up the mare and jumped off, but the hat dropped away to Loch Ryan. It would be a dangerously slick climb to retrieve it.

"Feck! Damn this bloody wind!" If Aunt Beatrice heard her speak such language, she'd rip every last hair from her head and slap her raw, but Morrigan went on spouting the words she often heard her brother and his comrades use. That hat was her favorite.

There it lay, on a narrow stretch of beach, against a stone. A grey seal gave it a curious sniff before tidewater reached out, grabbed it, and dragged the wretched thing into the loch.

Premonition crawled through her spine. The seal gazed up at her.

Come to me.

Morrigan pivoted in a breathless circle. There was nothing but waving grass, gorse, and thistle.

I need you.

She closed her eyes, hard, and when she opened them, gasped at the shimmering, almost transparent image of a man standing where the seal had been. His white knee-length tunic, topped by a leather cuirass, fluttered at the hem. Sunlight glinted against the hilt of a sword at his waist. One hand rested on his chest, and waving golden hair framed an uncompromising, sun-bronzed face. He seemed to stare directly at her.

The sea claims final possession, and leaves nothing behind.

Morrigan clapped her hands over her ears, shut her eyes, and counted to ten. When she opened them, she saw nothing but bright sunlight and a network of spider web clouds. There was the seal, rubbing its nose with one flipper. Loch Ryan washed against the shore and a curlew called sadly. It was a typical country scene, no different from a hundred other mornings.

She'd heard no voice. Wind, swirling through weeds, had fooled her. As if in confirmation, the seal barked as seals do, not sounding remotely human, and slid into the sea.

For years Morrigan had wondered if other people dreamed like she did, of places, people, and events that often left her twisting in her bedclothes and waking in a sweat. She never asked, for she was too afraid of being locked away in some ghastly place with mad folk.

She'd heard those words before, but never so clearly. She'd dreamed of that man, too, with his long golden hair and green eyes. They could be pitiless or tender, depending on his mood. *Theseus,* she'd long ago started calling him: magnificent, larger-than-life barbarian from Greek fable. Whenever she experienced the dream, she longed for...something. Her arms felt empty. Her heart ached. She knew none of it was real, but the beloved dream gave comfort, something to wish for.

She could almost believe, though she'd never even been kissed, that out there in the enormous, fathomless world, love waited. Impatient, ardent love. It came from a honey-haired man, who searched for her, called to her, spoke to her deepest recesses. When, *if*, he found her, he would snatch her out of this unhappy life. He would give her a castle with turrets that punctured the clouds. She would be safe. He would banish the demons from her soul.

The sea had sucked away her hat, but Morrigan felt it would like to seize her as well, yank her into its abysmal, inscrutable reaches.

Come to me, her dream-lover urged. *I've waited so long*.

Oh, find me, her heart cried. *I need you, too!*

Curran Ramsay stifled a sigh of boredom. How he'd managed to get roped into being Isabel MacLean's traveling companion quite escaped him. Somehow she'd contrived it, the moment she'd glimpsed him yesterday at the Glasgow station and waved her handkerchief, screeching to draw his attention. He remembered having a fondness for her, and he hadn't seen her in…well, he couldn't remember the last time. He knew her husband had died. No doubt she was lonely. He should invite her to Kilgarry for a change of scene. But she never stopped talking, and this morning, he found listening to her with the required expression of interest almost too exhausting to bear.

If only they'd met some other day. He would have dealt with it in a much more gentlemanly fashion. Today, however, he was thickheaded, bleary after a night of disruptions, moments of rest interrupted by long stretches of a persistent dream, or nightmare. He'd spent most of the night tossing and turning, and had to lock his jaw to keep from yawning in her face.

He'd planned to hide behind a copy of the *Dundee Courier* and spend the journey dismembering the dream. It always began with a spiraling sensation, like he'd been pushed into a hole or over a cliff, and was falling end over end. Then he would see himself carrying a child up out of the ground, a young girl bleeding profusely from a wound in the stomach. The staircase seemed endless, the girl's eyes huge in a pinched little face, and his feet were so heavy he could hardly lift them. He always kissed her forehead in an effort to reassure her, and to hide how terrified he was that she might expire in his arms. Sometimes the dream ended there as he hurtled out of sleep, gasping. Other times it continued, with him running into a large open space, being surrounded by men and women, all shouting in a language he couldn't begin to understand. They'd rip the child from him and carry her away, leaving him trapped by soldiers, who held sharp blades against his throat.

That particular dream never went any farther. He never knew if the child lived or died. Maybe it was the not knowing that filled him with this awful sense of guilt.

"I sold the gown to the lady and she showed it to her kin and acquaintances. I have so many orders coming in I may have to hire an assistant. What d'you think of that, Mr. Ramsay?"

"What? Oh...aye, Mrs. Maclean, it's bonny news. You'll soon be designing ballgowns for the royal family."

Her gaze narrowed, making him fear he'd said something wrong. "I swear you look as though you've lost your home and livelihood. Where is it you're off to, again?"

With determined effort, he smiled. "Larne, Mrs. Maclean, to buy a puppy. The owner has promised to hold the best of the litter for me. And what of you? You said you're traveling to Stranraer?"

As easily distracted as a two-year-old, she said, "Aye, to visit my brother, my nephew, and my niece. My brother is Douglas Lawton. He's an innkeeper now, you might recall. Your papa arranged for the fee, mind?"

"Of course, I do remember Mr. Lawton. I hope they are well?"

"Indeed they are. Thank you for asking."

The time passed sluggishly as Mrs. Maclean waxed into ecstatic descriptions of how breathtaking her niece had become and what a prodigy she was with music. "She first sat at a piano when she was three," Isabel claimed, "and played complex pieces of music by simply listening to others perform. It's truly astounding." She continued with stories of her braw young nephew, and how desperately frustrated she was by her brother's refusal to allow his children any of the finer graces in life. He'd even cut off Morrigan's music instruction, though Isabel was the one paying for it. It was a crime against art! She told Curran she often traveled to Stranraer to give the wee things a diversion from their perpetual chores. Douglas treated them like servants, slaves, or hired hands, and she was not exaggerating.

He forced himself to pay attention, to nod, smile, agree when it was needed, and to show the proper concern at the dreary life her niece and nephew were forced to live. His memories of Douglas Lawton's children were blurry; all he could picture was a vague image of his mother fawning over the infant.

"Is that hurting, Mr. Ramsay?" She pointed to the scar by his eye. "You're rubbing it rather vigorously."

He hadn't realized. The scar did hurt. Truthfully, he could hardly see through the haze of pain, and drew his fingers away prepared for blood, but there wasn't any. He couldn't remember the last time the old wound had caused such discomfort—not for years, not since the attack in the desolate wilds up by Loch Torridon. He'd always been self-conscious about the disfigurement, though it wasn't so bad—a simple defect that sliced through the outer edge of his left eyebrow and curved in a crescent shape past his eye to end at the top of his cheekbone. Women seemed to find it fascinating.

This had been a long journey. He was tired, and would be grateful to get home again. Maybe it was the pain that caused him to voice such an ignorant statement. As soon as the words left his mouth, he wished he could unsay them, but, of course, it was too late.

"I am lost, Mrs. Maclean. I often have this feeling, but it's much worse today." As he spoke, he thought of the other dream, for it, too, involved a scar. In this dream, he held a woman. He lifted her hand and turned it, kissing an odd, reddish mark on the inside of her wrist, a scar of some kind, or a blemish left by an old burn. The woman pulled him closer, saying, *Kiss me. Kiss me again.* He never could recall her face when he woke, though he spent countless hours trying, and couldn't be sure if this was someone he knew, or a fabrication shaped wholly in his head.

Simply thinking of it made his heart speed up and shortened his breathing. He turned away from the prim and proper Isabel MacLean, carefully refolding the newspaper on his lap while tamping down an almost overwhelming erotic hunger.

Thankfully, before she had a chance to give him stern, common-sense platitudes about the healing power of tea and toast, and how one must never eat cheese before bed, or how he needed a wife to be happy, the train whistle blared, disintegrating the last remnants of desire.

They'd arrived in Stranraer.

The Sixth Labyrinth
CHAPTER TWO

"Morrigan! Morrigan Lawton!"

An insistent, rather braying voice carried over the rush and bustle of busy townsfolk, arriving passengers, and resting growl of the train engine. Reining in Widdie, Morrigan glanced over her shoulder.

"Here...over here!"

A white square handkerchief waved, vanished behind a group of tall, solemn-frocked gentlemen, then reappeared as they passed.

She squinted. A short, squat woman, dwarfed by an enormous feathered hat. Why, it was Aunt Isabel, Papa's sister from the Highlands.

Morrigan wheeled her mount. She'd be even later getting home, but it couldn't be helped. Maybe the arrival of his only sister would soothe Papa's anger.

As Morrigan dismounted, brushing hair out of her eyes, Isabel pulled her into an exuberant, perfumed hug, released her, and gave her a thorough examination, going so far as to turn her niece in a circle.

"Where is your hat? How many times must I remind you that a lady never goes out with her head uncovered? And will you look at this? We'll be hours on these snarls. You're seventeen, Morrigan, a lady of marriageable—"

"Eighteen, Auntie, I'm halfway to nineteen—"

"Old enough to mind a hat, then. I've made you enough to suit a countess. Surely one of them appeals. There is simply no excuse. Why has Beatrice allowed you to ride out half dressed?"

Humiliation burned Morrigan's cheeks as the last departing passengers sent varying glances of disapproval or amusement her way. Aunt Isabel's voice tended to carry.

"I left before she woke up. And I love the hats you've made me, Aunt Ibby. I love them, truly."

"You need to spend more time with that lass, what's her name... Enid. She could teach you a thing or two about the habits of a proper lady."

Morrigan sighed. Enid Joyce was blessed with wealth, an impressive home, and, as she often boasted, an introduction to the queen's youngest daughter. Her finest accomplishment in Morrigan's opinion was a tongue so sour it could blacken a pickle, and she used it freely to belittle others. Aunt Isabel, forced to take up a trade after the death of her husband, had become a seamstress, and did quite well. For years, she'd showered her niece with fine, hand-sewn clothing. This had drawn Enid's scrutiny to one she never would have deigned to notice otherwise. Over the last three years or so, Stranraer's bachelor gentlemen had begun to openly admire the innkeeper's daughter, they being so much less discriminating than Enid. In response, Enid's castigation had escalated into the righteous outrage of the wellborn against peasants who dared ape their betters.

Morrigan thought it best to move on to another topic. "Does Papa know you've come?"

"No." Isabel's stern expression melted into an unpretentious smile. "It's a surprise. I've brought a friend, and he's fair anxious to meet you. Now where's that lad gone off to? He was right behind me a moment ago."

Morrigan's thorn-pricked finger stung. She stuck it in her mouth, tasting bitter remnants of yellow gorse and the slightest mineral hint of blood.

"Did you see where my traveling companion went?" Isabel asked a nearby porter.

"No, mum." The man was blandly polite, yet Morrigan caught the brief narrowing of his eyes, the flicker of annoyance. *I have no idea who your companion is, and moreover, I do not care*, his frown suggested.

Isabel, oblivious to such subtleties, replied tartly, "Well, help me find him. We don't have all day to stand about. And where is my trunk?"

The porter half-ran to keep up with Isabel's rotund figure as she hurried along the platform, chastising him all the way.

"She's a remarkable lady, your aunt."

Morrigan turned towards the nearest car. A figure stood there, still and dark, little more than an outline. The fine hairs along the edge of her scalp lifted, and she hastily removed her finger from her mouth, tucking it behind her. "Aye," she replied.

"You must be Miss Lawton." His voice reminded her of the way barley whispered in warm breezes.

Thinking something had gone wrong with her sight, she blinked. A mist of color surrounded the being on the step, like a rainbow glimmering through watery clouds, but this rainbow offered only the blue spectrum, with hints of violet.

She managed to contain a desire to reach out and ruffle the colors like the surface of a pool. "I am," she said, taking a half-step backward. There was nothing to fear. She heard her aunt berating the porter a few cars away. Nevertheless.... She lifted one brow. "How d'you know that, sir?"

"Forgive me." He descended the steps. A shaft of sunlight, finding its way through a hole in the station's wood and glass ceiling, pinned him in a halo of light.

For one instant that seemed unending, the world stopped. The train engine's pant faded into the overpowering pulse of her blood.

"Beg your pardon, Miss Lawton?"

The words sank into her brain as though slogging through mud. "Wha-what?"

"Did you say, 'Theseus'?"

For an instant more, she remained trapped in muffling cotton. Then the world burst apart. Her heart lurched. A surge, what a lightning bolt must feel like, streaked through her, almost drawing her up on tiptoe, as though she'd lain dormant her whole life until now. She wasn't at all certain her heart could handle the strain. Along with a thousand other mental pictures, gone too quick to make any sense of, she saw herself clutch her chest, fall, and expire, right before the physical embodiment of her long-cherished illusion.

A breeze lifted his unruly blond hair, fair begging for a woman's smoothing hand. Supple skin, mouth curving on one side, bringing out a playful dimple. Alert twilight blue eyes beneath dark brows, hinting at confidences and merriment he'd like to share. Clean-shaven. Five and twenty? Older perhaps, the direct gaze and confident stance hinted; maybe younger, said the unlined skin, riotous hair and generous mouth.

Her frozen muscles grew hot and began to tremble. *Daftie. He's a man, not a Greek hero come to life.*

"Miss Lawton, are you well?" He stepped closer, lifting a hand as though in contemplation of grasping her shoulder.

Her gaze locked on a scar marring his otherwise perfect face, curving around his left eye. It was shaped like a miniature crescent moon, or one of those Moslem curved swords: a scimitar. "Aye, I'm well, Mr.—Mr.?"

"Ramsay." He inclined his head. "Curran Ramsay."

"You're the...my aunt's traveling companion?"

"I had that pleasure, aye."

"There you are, Mr. Ramsay." Isabel's voice intruded with the hearty insistence of a magpie. "I've located our bags. Have you met my niece?"

"If this young lady is your niece, Mrs. Maclean."

Throughout her aunt's dialogue, Mr. Ramsay kept his gaze on Morrigan. The undisguised admiration in those vivid blue eyes helped her dismiss the notion that in her many ardent reveries, she had always created her hero with eyes of green. She supposed she was like most females, and couldn't resist a man canny enough to reveal his appreciation.

The strange colors that had sparkled around him were gone, banished perhaps by the light of the sun. He smiled as though he and Morrigan shared some private, affectionate joke about Aunt Ibby, and Morrigan's knees turned to butter. The smile was angelic, yet to charm her so, it must be diabolical. She clamped down on her wayward thoughts, fearful of spouting more half-witted nonsense. *Theseus.* For the sake of blessed pity, had she really said that out loud?

"And is she not all I claimed?"

"Indeed, Mrs. Maclean, you failed to do her justice."

Morrigan glanced from the gentleman to her smirking aunt and thought her cheeks might erupt in flames.

"Mr. Ramsay's an acquaintance of yours, my dear, though you couldn't possibly remember. He hails from Glenelg."

She returned her scrutiny to him. Light glanced off his gold tiepin, a fancy scrolled "CR," one wee diamond separating the two letters.

No, she could not have actually met and forgotten this sun god, the male who'd haunted her daydreams for as long as she'd been alive. Everything about him seemed to shout, *I am here to rescue you.*

She cleared her throat. "Aye?" Her voice sounded faint and tinny through the drumbeat of blood in her ears. *Theseus.* In the flesh. The golden dream-lover.

Yet he wasn't exactly the same. His hair wasn't nearly as long, and he was dressed like any other proper gentleman, in striped trousers, tie, and waistcoat, not in leather armor and greaves. She nearly laughed out loud as she imagined what would happen in conservative Stranraer if a man stepped off the train adorned in such a costume. Now that she put cold logic to it, she realized he didn't resemble the hero in her fantasy, really, except for the color of his hair. She must have been half asleep, still floating in her dream spell, to think it. The stench of acrid smoke, windblown rubbish, and sullen porters were returning her to common sense and drab reality.

There was no denying though, that part of her longed for him to exclaim his own happy knowledge, to clasp her in his arms and refuse to let her go.

But he merely bowed like every other gentleman she'd ever been introduced to. "Pleased to meet you, Miss Lawton."

"And I you, Mr. Ramsay." She'd never worked so hard to keep her voice steady.

Isabel tugged Morrigan towards the street. "Will you join us, Mr. Ramsay? Come and break your fast at my brother's inn."

"I'd love to," he said.

She gave the porter detailed instructions on what to do with their luggage then swept towards Stranraer proper, heels clicking on the cobblestones. "D'you care if we walk?" she asked. "It's only a bit up the road and I feel the need to stretch my legs."

"Certainly." Mr. Ramsay took Widdie's reins and offered Morrigan his arm. His left brow came up, causing two horizontal lines to crease his forehead, and elongating the crescent scar.

What would it be like…to touch it?

She curled her hand obediently around his forearm, hoping he couldn't feel her nervousness through his coat sleeve.

Enid Joyce, enthroned on the seat of a shining victoria drawn by two matched bays, chose that moment to pass. Her well-fitted jacket, strung with lace, accented an hourglass figure. Blue eyes, beneath a head of perfectly coiffed hair, narrowed as the lass observed her rival so neatly ensconced on the arm of this handsome stranger.

Morrigan had almost forgotten her shortcomings beneath Ramsay's admiring regard. Now she remembered her bare head, snarled braid, and bitten fingernails. Her homespun dress, still littered with a few stubborn stickseeds and patches of dust, offered evidence of her time in the wild, and she was sure she smelled of horse. Next to Enid's slim figure, Morrigan felt as cumbersome as an elephant seal. She shriveled, much like a blossom left too long without water.

Of course Aunt Isabel had to pause and say good morning. Enid replied with easy smiling grace, as though she and Morrigan were life-long comrades. The lass displayed her saucy dimple and for good measure fluttered long black lashes as she extended a hand encased in a lace-trimmed glove.

"Now there's a born lady," Isabel said as Enid ordered her driver on. "See how her parasol draws attention to her hat? You'd never catch *her* without a hat."

Perhaps she noticed how her niece flinched, for she patted Morrigan's shoulder, adding, "Still, you've a charm she lacks. I cannot put a name to it, really…." She gave their companion a roguish wink. "Don't you agree, sir?"

"Aye, indeed," he replied. "A most intriguing and singular charm."

Isabel's face exuded satisfaction, and Morrigan realized what was truly going on. Her aunt had dragged this poor, unsuspecting fellow here, using trickery, no doubt, for the sole purpose of meeting her. She'd die if he perceived he was being paraded as a candidate for marriage. His fine suit proclaimed his wealth and his manner of speech almost screamed *expensive education*. Heaven knew what Isabel thought he'd find appealing in a penniless innkeeper's daughter who'd only been allowed eight years in an unpolished, rural school.

She lowered her face to hide her mortification.

Aunt Isabel would drag Crown Prince Edward himself to Morrigan's door if she could manage it. Aye, she would.

And no doubt she would expect the prince to display humble appreciation over his good fortune, since he was, after all, naught but a damned Englishman.

THE SIXTH LABYRINTH
BOOK FIVE
Available Everywhere in digital and paperback

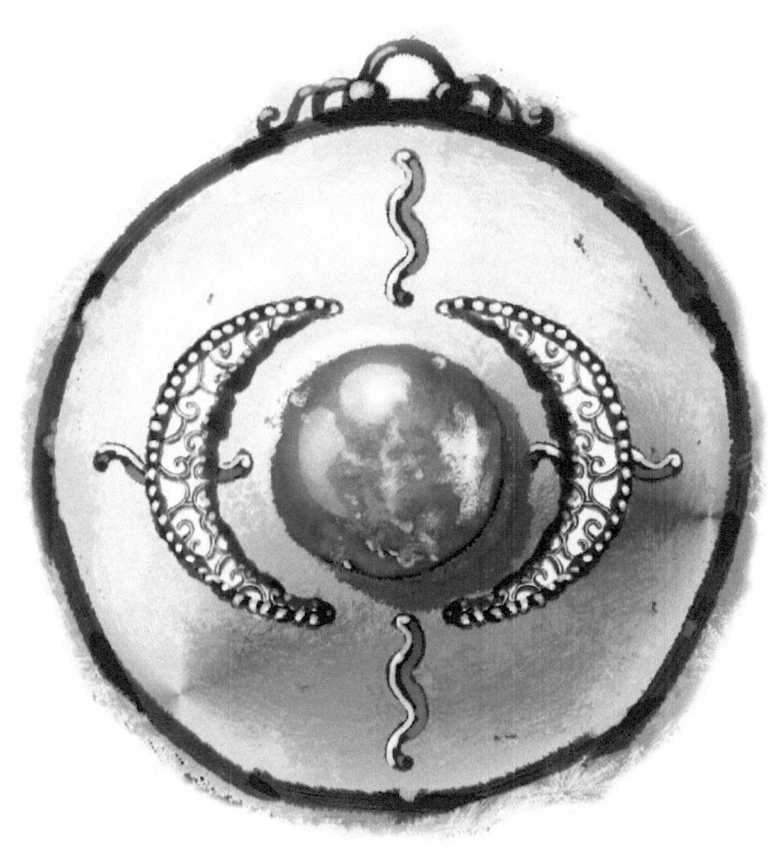